PRACTICE
MAKES
PERFECT

PRACTICE MAKES PERFECT

a **VARSITY** *novel*

by Melanie Spring

poppy

Little, Brown and Company
New York Boston

Copyright © 2014 by Varsity Spirit Corporation
Varsity is a registered trademark of Varsity Spirit Corporation.

Poppy

Hachette Book Group
237 Park Avenue, New York, NY 10017
Visit our website at lb-teens.com

Poppy is an imprint of Little, Brown and Company.
The Poppy name and logo are trademarks of Hachette Book Group, Inc.

The publisher is not responsible for websites (or their content)
that are not owned by the publisher.

First Edition: September 2014

Library of Congress Cataloging-in-Publication Data
Spring, Melanie.
Practice makes perfect : a Varsity novel / by Melanie Spring. — First edition.
    pages cm
"Poppy" — Copyright page.
Sequel to: Turn it up.
Summary: "The pressure is on as JV cheerleaders Chloe, Devin, Kate, and Emily practice Varsity-level stunts, amidst the drama of best friends, boyfriends, and frenemies" — Provided by publisher.
ISBN 978-0-316-22733-9 (trade pbk.) — ISBN 978-0-316-36510-9 (library edition ebook) — ISBN 978-0-316-22732-2 (ebook) [1. Cheerleading—Fiction.   2. Best friends—Fiction.
3. Friendship—Fiction.   4. Dating (Social customs)—Fiction.   5. High schools—Fiction.
6. Schools—Fiction.]   I. Title.
    PZ7.S76843Pr 2014   [Fic]—dc23   2013048075

10 9 8 7 6 5 4 3 2 1

RRD-C

Printed in the United States of America

CHAPTER 1

Devin Isle sprinted into the Northside High gym, her curly red mane flying behind her. Practice had started five minutes earlier, and she knew how Coach Steele felt about tardiness—along with tattoos, press-on nails, and the other no-no's in the Junior Varsity Cheerleader Contract.

This was *not* a good way to begin the tryout season.

"Guys! Where's Coach? Am I in trouble?" Devin called out to her friends Chloe Davis, Emily Arellano, and Kate MacDonald. The three girls were warming up on the mats along with the rest of their squad. Devin paused to catch her breath and dig through her duffel bag for a hair elastic.

"Twenty demerits!" Emily joked, her brown eyes sparkling.

She grabbed her right elbow and stretched it over her head. "Actually, twenty-one, if you count the fact that your socks don't match."

"What?" Devin glanced at her feet in alarm. How had she managed to put on one plain sock and one Hello Kitty sock? It wouldn't really cost her a demerit, but still. She was usually more organized than that.

"Don't worry, Devin. Coach isn't even here yet," Kate reassured her. She tied a neat white ribbon around her light brown hair, frowned, and retied the bow. "I have an extra pair of ankle socks, if you want to borrow them," she added.

"Thanks, Kate!"

"So where were you?" Chloe asked Devin. As always, Chloe looked like the quintessential cheerleader: sleek strawberry-blond ponytail with neat bangs, blue NHS CHEER T-shirt, and gold camp shorts. And, of course, matching cheer socks.

"My mom locked herself out of the house. So I had to run home really fast and let her in," Devin explained.

"Oh. Booooring. I thought that maybe you were in a lip-lock with your BF and lost track of time," Emily said, wiggling her eyebrows.

Kate gasped in shock. *"Emily!"*

Chloe giggled.

Devin blushed furiously. "Mateo is *not* my boyfriend. He's just a good friend."

"Well, I wish *I* had a 'good friend' like him," Emily said, making quote marks with her fingers. "He's hot!" Emily was single at the moment, which was a rare relationship status for her. She was the most boy-crazy girl Devin had ever met.

The shrill sound of a whistle pierced the gym. Devin, Emily, Kate, and Chloe automatically jumped to attention, along with the fourteen other JV cheerleaders.

Coach Steele strolled through the double doors. She wore her usual navy-blue warm-ups with a gold accent down the sleeves, and her silver whistle dangled around her neck on an NHS lanyard. "Gather around, my little Timberwolves!" she called out. "I have some announcements to make before we get started!"

Everyone rushed to form a wide semicircle in front of her and sat down cross-legged on the polished wooden floor. The coach sipped from a silver coffee thermos and did a slow scan around the gym. Her eyes seemed to linger on something or someone in the distance.

Devin turned. Just past the bleachers, Principal Cilento stood in the doorway with a man in a teal polo and neatly pressed khakis. Devin didn't recognize him.

Coach Steele set her thermos aside and fixed her attention on the girls. Her expression softened into a proud smile. "First of all, happy Tuesday!" she said loudly. "As many of you already know, today marks the beginning of our new practice schedule. Basketball season is officially over. Nationals are behind us—and, may I add, you ladies rocked that competition. Fifth place! Not fifth in the city of Sunny Valley. Not fifth in the state of California. But fifth *in the entire country!*"

The squad broke out in wild applause. "Timber! Timber! Timber-wolves!" Chloe shouted, pumping her fist in the air. The other girls joined in.

Coach Steele nodded at the group of bright, shiny faces. Then she raised her hands, and everyone immediately fell silent.

"For the next five weeks, we will be practicing on Tuesdays and Thursdays only, and these practices will be required only for those of you who are trying out for next year," she went on. "We will *not* be learning new routines or refining our old ones. We will focus solely on preparing for tryouts. I've just confirmed the dates with Principal Cilento. There will be two days of clinics on Monday, April seventh, and Tuesday, April eighth, right after school. At the clinics, you will be learning your tryout routine, among other things. Then tryouts will be on Wednesday, April ninth, also after school."

Leila Savett flipped her long black hair over her shoulders. "But Coach, why do we have to try out? We're already on the squad," she complained.

"I totally agree with Leila," Marcy Martinez piped up.

Marcy's nickname was "Savett's Shadow" because she followed Leila everywhere and echoed whatever she said.

"Thank you for sharing your opinions with us, Savett and Martinez," Coach Steele said drily. "But none of you is guaranteed a spot on next year's JV squad just because you're on it this year. Each and every one of you has to prove to me and to the judges at tryouts that you deserve to continue. Furthermore, some of you may be ready to move up to the Varsity team. The only way we can determine that is for you to show us what you've got on April ninth."

Everyone began buzzing and whispering.

"And don't forget—you won't just be competing against each other," Coach Steele went on. "There will be a whole slew of incoming freshmen from Jefferson and Los Gatos middle schools who will be trying out, too."

"Eighth graders, ha!" Leila muttered, rolling her ice-blue eyes. "They don't stand a chance against us."

Devin frowned at Leila's comment. Leila had been in eighth grade only a year ago—the same as Devin, Emily, Kate, and Chloe, and most of the other girls present. Who did she think she was, making fun of the younger kids?

Of course, Leila *was* Leila. Last fall, the girl had resorted to lies, rumors, and fake e-mails to try to make Devin and Chloe hate each other and step down from their roles as cocaptains of the JV squad. Fortunately, Devin and Chloe had seen through Leila's ruse. They'd continued to lead the squad together—all the way to Regionals and Nationals, and, of course, at dozens of games, practices, and pep rallies.

It hadn't been easy. But Devin and Chloe had done it. And now the two of them were not only cocaptains but also friends. Maybe not *best* friends, exactly, but friends nevertheless.

Devin raised her hand. "Coach Steele? Are there separate clinics and tryouts for JV and Varsity?" she asked.

A few of the other girls gave her a look like she was nuts. Devin squirmed, feeling a little awkward. She had never actually been through cheerleading clinics *or* tryouts. Six months ago, when Devin was a new student at Northside, Coach Steele had just put her on the JV squad without a tryout. Some of the cheerleaders had not been happy about that, including Chloe.

Coach Steele used to coach Sage, Devin's older sister, back when both the Isle family and the coach had lived up in the Bay Area. Sage Isle had been a household name in the world of high school cheerleading; she'd led Spring Park High to Nationals and been featured in *American Cheerleader* magazine. Sage was now a sophomore and a cheerleader at UCLA.

When Devin and her mom, Linda, moved to Sunny Valley last summer, Coach Steele had personally recruited

Devin to be on the Northside JV cheer squad, in part because she was Sage's little sister, but also because of her advanced tumbling skills. Devin had agreed, mostly to make her mom happy.

At first, Devin had hated cheerleading. She'd never done a high V or a Herkie in her life; she was a gymnast, not a cheerleader. But slowly, gradually, she'd come around. And now, she couldn't imagine *not* being a cheerleader.

"To answer your question, Devin—it's just one process," Coach Steele replied. "Everyone will be trying out together: the incoming freshmen, JV cheerleaders, Varsity cheerleaders, and anyone else who is interested in joining the squad. You will *all* be performing the same cheers and dances on April ninth. However, those of you who want to be considered for Varsity will have to kick it up a notch with your tumbling and stunts."

"How?" a freshman named Jenn Hoffheimer asked.

"I'm glad you asked, Hoffheimer. For your standing tumbling requirement, a back handspring is a minimum for JV," Coach Steele explained. "For Varsity, you should be prepared to throw a standing back tuck or a standing back handspring tuck. For your running tumbling, we like to see a round-off back handspring for JV and a round-off, back handspring, tuck for Varsity. Furthermore, if you tried out last year with a certain skill, we want to see you try out with a more difficult skill this year. If you've lost that original skill altogether, that will be a huge minus on your score sheet."

She added, "As for stunts, you should aim for ones that will showcase your individual talents. For example, the Varsity squad had a ground-up liberty in their competition routine this year."

Yikes! Devin thought. The ground-up liberty was a challenging stunt. It involved the two bases and the spotter lifting the top girl into a stag position with one foot on her knee.

"But don't just focus on your tumbling and stunts," the coach went on. "At tryouts, we want to see clean, crisp motions and strong jumps. We want to see big smiles. We want to see that you can work together as a team. We want to see that you're able to engage the crowd."

"Coach Steele? Will the clinics be the same as they were last year?" a sophomore named Phoebe Carter asked.

"Yes. On day one, the graduating Varsity cheerleaders will be teaching you a brand-new tryout cheer and dance. On day two, you will get a chance to fine-tune them, and also practice your tumbling and stunts," Coach Steele replied. "By the way, you should be forming your stunt groups as soon as possible. And remember—you can be in more than one stunt group at tryouts. That can be a good way to demonstrate your range of talents. But you can only designate one stunt as your tryout stunt."

"We are totally going to be a stunt group," Emily whispered to Chloe, Kate, and Devin, who gave thumbs-up signs.

Coach Steele began pacing back and forth. "Finally, I want to say that tryouts are important—but in truth, this whole year has been a tryout. For the past six months and at cheer camp last summer, I've had a chance to watch your skills...your attitudes...how you interact with your squad mates...how you are at the games. This is your chance to build on that. From now until April ninth, you should work very, very hard to become even better. That means showing up here every Tuesday and Thursday. Also, please practice at home. Watch yourselves in a mirror. Make sure your motions are sharp. Work on those gorgeous smiles."

She stopped and regarded the girls. "Now, get off your behinds and get moving! Let's start with warm-ups, then line up for tumbling. On Thursday, we'll do some stunting."

The cheerleaders jumped to their feet and headed for the mats. Devin, Emily, Kate, and Chloe walked side by side. "I'm glad Coach explained all that," Kate said to the others. "I'm definitely going to go for the JV squad again. Varsity sounds cool, but I don't think I can learn to throw a tuck in five weeks. What about you guys?"

Devin took a sip from her water bottle. The Varsity tumbling requirements would not be a problem for her, but she didn't want to say that and sound like a show-off. "I think I'll go for Varsity when I'm a junior," she said after a moment. "It's a *huge* time commitment. I may want to do some other extracurricular stuff next year."

"Me, three," Emily said, smoothing her cheer shorts over her tanned legs. "We can all go for Varsity next spring!"

"Losers! I'm going for Varsity *this* spring," Leila announced smugly as she passed them.

"Well, so am I!" Chloe said quickly. She stared defiantly at Leila.

Devin blinked. Did Chloe really want to go for Varsity? Or was she just saying that to annoy her number one frenemy?

"Don't let Leila get to you, Chloe," Kate said as Leila walked away.

Chloe smiled brightly. "I'm not! Honestly, I don't care what Leila Savett does or doesn't do."

But as she stared after Leila, her smile disappeared.

What is Chloe up to? Devin wondered.

CHAPTER 2

"Okay, so the spring dance is on May third. Which means that we have two months to find a band or a DJ," Emily announced to Chloe.

"*We?*" Chloe repeated.

It was Wednesday after school, and Emily had invited Chloe to come over to her house. Chloe had assumed that they would study for Mr. Liu's quiz on marine ecosystems together and that the Arellanos would invite her to stay for dinner. Mr. Arellano always made meat loaf and mashed potatoes on Wednesday nights, which was one of Chloe's favorite meals. Chloe's own parents were working late; her dad's law firm was in the middle of a big trial, and her mom had an important house closing at her real estate company.

But somehow Emily had turned from coral reefs and salt marshes to the spring dance.

They were in Emily's room, which was decorated all in purples and yellows. Boy band posters covered the walls. Piles of fashion magazines and bottles of glittery nail polish cluttered her desk.

Emily cleared a swath on her bed, sending books, notebooks, and clothes cascading to the floor. She plucked one of the notebooks out of the mess. "Here it is!" The book was labeled SPRING DANCE COMMITTEE. "I've already written down some ideas. Like, what do you think about that band from Torrance Heights called Motion Sickness?"

Chloe perched on the edge of the bed and frowned skeptically at her friend. "Hey, Emily? *You're* on the spring dance committee, not me. I'm way too busy to get involved in anything else right now. I have, like, three huge papers to write before spring break. I spend every Saturday at Hearts Heal." Hearts Heal was a charity that assisted families in need. The JV squad had raised money for the group in the past, and Chloe had decided to do additional volunteer work there on her own. "And last but not least, there's tryouts," she added.

For a moment, Chloe thought about her spontaneous announcement that she was going to go for the Varsity squad. It meant that she would need to perfect a standing back tuck or a standing back handspring tuck in a little over a month—and a round-off, back handspring, tuck, too. Or better yet, upgrade to a round-off, back handspring, layout. Would she be able to nail these difficult moves in time?

Before yesterday, she hadn't actually decided between JV and Varsity for next year. But when Leila had declared her intention to try out for Varsity, Chloe had just… *reacted*. Leila Savett always had that effect on her. It was weird, especially since Chloe and Leila used to be really good friends. They'd hung out at each other's houses and carpooled to the mall. That was way back in elementary and middle school, before Chloe made the elite team at the Sunny Valley All-Stars gym and Leila didn't. Leila hadn't taken that well, and after that, their relationship had quickly deteriorated.

"I'm crazy-busy too," Emily said sympathetically. "I told the rest of the spring dance committee members that I would deal with the entertainment, but that's it. No making flyers and posters, no shopping for decorations, no baking cookies." She added, "I thought it would be fun for you and me to look for bands and DJs together. You have such awesome taste in music."

"I do?"

"You do! Remember when you made that playlist for Will Resnick in sixth grade? It was epic!"

Chloe hugged her knees to her chest and laughed. Leave it to Emily to bring up something from a zillion years ago. The two girls, along with Kate, had been best friends since forever.

"Yeah, but Will Resnick didn't think my playlist was so epic. He asked Ashley Cummings to be his girlfriend instead of me," Chloe reminded Emily.

"Minor detail. The point is, you and I should totally do this. A subcommittee of two. Super-exclusive. Let's take a vote. All in favor?" Emily raised her hand. She reached over and lifted Chloe's hand for her. "It's unanimous! Now, let's get started...."

Chloe sighed. Emily was impossible—and impossible to say no to. "Okay, *fiiine*! What do we have to do?"

Emily sat up with a happy grin. "I'm glad you asked! So first, we need to make a list of bands and DJs that we want to consider. Then we'll contact them and ask them for their demos."

"I'm guessing we won't be contacting Hashtag, then, right?" Chloe asked curiously.

Emily's grin vanished, and she scrunched up her nose. Hashtag was a band consisting of three Northside juniors: Travis Hollister, Alex Guzmann, and Kyle Klein. Emily used to be their on-again, off-again female vocalist. And just recently, a record company called Rampage had shown interest in signing up Hashtag for their label.

Emily had almost given up cheerleading for the chance to become a professional singer. She'd also been Travis's sort-of girlfriend for a while. But eventually she'd decided to stick with the JV squad. On the same day she'd told Travis the news, he'd broken up with her.

"Grrrr. No, Hashtag is *not* on the list," Emily said irritably.

"I'm sorry I brought it up," Chloe apologized.

"It's okay. Hashtag is history. Let's move on." Emily flipped through the pages of her notebook. "So I really like Motion Sickness a lot. And this girl band called Psycho Bunnies. Oh, and what do you think about that DJ we had for the Valentine's Day dance? You know, Eddie's friend Mad Dog?" Eddie was one of Emily's older brothers.

"Yeah, he was pretty good. Isn't Luisa Kessler's uncle a DJ, too?"

"No, it's Luisa's *cousin*, but I heard he's crazy-expensive...."

Chloe and Emily continued to chat about possible candidates, as the yummy smell of meat loaf and mashed potatoes wafted up from the kitchen. Outside the window, the twilight sky turned purple and pink. A big family minivan pulled into the driveway; it was probably Mrs. Arellano, home from her job as a preschool teacher.

At five thirty, someone knocked on Emily's door. Her other brother Chris poked his head in. He was a senior, a

Varsity football and basketball player, and one of the most popular guys at Northside.

"Dinner in ten," he announced. "Oh, hey, Chlo! You're eating with us, right? Did you get a haircut? Looks cute." With that, he disappeared down the hall.

Chloe felt her cheeks flush. Chris had never given her a compliment—ever. She had known him for years, from the time she was an awkward wannabe cheerleader with pink-tinted braces. In her eyes, Chris Arellano had always been Emily's big brother and nothing more.

"What haircut?" Emily asked, confused. "Did you go to Stylistics and not tell me? What kind of friend are you?"

"I didn't get a haircut. I started using this new mango conditioner, though. It's supposed to add shine and body. Maybe my hair looks different?" Chloe reached up and fluffed her bangs. "So what's going on with Chris? Does he have a girlfriend these days? Or is he single?" she asked casually.

Emily stared at Chloe. "No!"

"No, he doesn't have a girlfriend? Or no, he's not single?"

"No, you are *not* going to date my brother," Emily said firmly. "First of all—*eww!* Second of all, I thought you liked that boy from Sunny Valley Performing Arts. Gemma Moore's brother. Daniel, right?"

"Daniel and I decided we were better as just friends," Chloe replied. "And I'm *not* going to date Chris! He's a senior! I was curious, that's all."

"I don't believe you. You have that look in your eyes."

"What look in my eyes?"

"The same look you had in eighth grade when you said you didn't like Greg Marina, and you totally did, and see how *that* turned out?"

"He picked Leila over me. Thanks for the reminder. Now, let's get back to the spring dance. Why don't I research local bands and DJs online?"

As Chloe pulled her new iPad out of her backpack, she thought about Chris Arellano's chocolate-brown eyes. And dimples. And lean, athletic build.

Why had she never noticed him before?

"Thank you, Mrs. Arellano!" Chloe said, waving.

Chloe crossed her front yard as Emily and her mother drove away. It was a warm evening, and palm fronds swayed gently in the balmy breeze. The Davises lived in one of the nicest neighborhoods in Sunny Valley. Large mansions lined their street, landscaped with bright tropical flowers, garden fountains, infinity pools, and koi ponds.

Chloe had almost reached the front door when she heard someone calling her name. She turned and saw her neighbor Jasmyn Gibbs running up to her. Behind Jasmyn was a girl Chloe didn't recognize. They were both dressed in Jefferson Middle School T-shirts and denim short shorts.

"Chloe! Hi!" Jasmyn chirped. "This is my friend Beatrice!"

Beatrice waved and smiled shyly. She had short brown hair and lots of freckles.

"Hey, Jasmyn! Nice to meet you, Beatrice," Chloe said.

Jasmyn twirled one of her mini-braids around and around her index finger. "Guess what? We're going to try out for the Northside cheer club!" she announced.

"That's awesome!" Chloe said with a nod. She didn't add that it was called a cheer *squad*, not club. "It's *so* much fun being a cheerleader!"

"The thing is...we were wondering...maybe...could you help us practice?" Jasmyn asked.

Beatrice nodded, her brown eyes wide.

"Like a couple of times a week, after school? Or on weekends? We'll even pay you out of our babysitting money!" Jasmyn went on.

Beatrice continued nodding.

"Oh!" Chloe hesitated. "I wish I could! The thing is, I've got a lot going on right now. But I could let you borrow some of Jake and Clem's old training videos, if you'd like?" Chloe's older twin siblings, college seniors, were legendary members of the Northside Varsity squad.

Jasmyn and Beatrice's faces fell.

"Sure. That's okay. We just thought we'd ask! See you around, Chloe. Go, Timberwolves!" Jasmyn jumped up in the air and attempted a double toe touch. Beatrice did the same.

They failed miserably—and landed in a heap on the Davises' lawn.

Chloe rushed to help them to their feet. "Are you guys all right?" she asked worriedly.

"We're fine!" Jasmyn said, looking embarrassed. "Timber, Timber, Timber—"

"—wolves!" Beatrice squeaked.

As the two girls walked back to Jasmyn's house, Chloe felt a twinge of guilt. Cheerleading had taught her the importance of helping others. Was she being selfish by not helping Jasmyn and Beatrice?

CHAPTER 3

Emily hurried down Figueroa Street, trying not to trip in her new peep-toe platforms that showed off the glittery blue pedicure she'd given herself last night. It was a beautiful Saturday morning, and downtown Sunny Valley was crowded. The sidewalks were packed with joggers, couples on brunch dates, and parents with strollers. Emily recognized some seniors from Northside, who were hanging out on the patio at the Mighty Cup, where her brother Eddie worked.

Her phone buzzed. She pulled it out of her bag and glanced at the screen. It was a text from Devin:

Do u want to go to the park and practice for tryouts? I tried Chloe and Kate, too, but they're volunteering at Hearts Heal today.

Emily typed:

Wish I could! But I'm starting my new job this morning!

Devin replied:

What new job??????

Emily wrote:

Rockabella Boutique. Wish me luck. Gotta run. TTYL!

Emily slipped her phone back into her bag. Ironically, the phone—which she'd nicknamed "Chad"—was one of the reasons she'd gotten the part-time job to begin with. Chad was ancient. Its screen was cracked and Emily couldn't even video chat. With the money she would make at Rockabella over the next few months, she would be able to retire Chad and buy an upgrade, preferably a sleek white iPhone. She even had a hot-pink case in mind. It had a picture of a megaphone on it and the phrase KEEP CALM AND CHEER ON.

A minute later, Emily strolled through the front door of Rockabella. It had always been one of her favorite boutiques in Sunny Valley, and now she would be an employee there. How cool was that? She'd gotten to know the owner, Nadine Rodriguez, after helping to organize the JV squad's fashion show fund-raiser back in January. Nadine had donated a cute red maxi dress that had sold for a hundred dollars during the live auction. In fact, the fund-raiser was why Emily had decided to get a job at a clothing store versus, say, the Mighty Cup or Swirls or Disc-O-Rama. She liked coffee, fro-yo, and vinyl. But she liked clothes even more, whether it was wearing them or working with them.

"You're late."

Emily stopped in her tracks. Her new boss stood in front of the cash register, her arms crossed over her chest and her mouth drawn in a thin, angry line. Nadine was dressed all in black—silk blouse, skinny jeans, and cowboy boots—accented with tons of silver-and-turquoise jewelry. Her long black hair was streaked dramatically with a single strand of gray.

Emily peered at her watch. "I...uh...my shift doesn't start until ten, right? It's nine fifty-seven now," she said, confused.

"You should always be here ten minutes early. Anything after that is late as far as I'm concerned. Why aren't you dressed?" Nadine demanded.

"Excuse me?"

"That...*outfit*. If you can call it that. You need to appear stylish and sophisticated if you expect customers to value your opinion about clothes. Rockabella is a house of fashion, not a house of thrift-store leftovers."

Emily felt heat rush to her cheeks as she gazed down at her favorite denim skirt, white lace peasant top, and beaded necklace. She'd based the outfit on one she'd recently seen in a magazine spread. "I'm sorry! I'll—uh—change! Right now! I can go home and be back in—um—twenty minutes!" she stammered.

Nadine narrowed her pale blue eyes. "And be even later than you already are? I don't think so. You can do work in the back room today. We just got in a new shipment of prom dresses. You can steam out the wrinkles and hang them up. You do know how to use a garment steamer, right?"

"Yes! Of course!" At this point, Emily would have said yes even if she *didn't* know how to use one. "I'll do a good job, I promise!"

"Let *me* be the judge of that," Nadine said coldly.

Emily gulped. Nadine Rodriguez was definitely the most frightening person she'd ever met.

The front door opened, and a girl waltzed in, carrying a tray of coffees from Mighty Cup. She wore a form-fitting black jersey dress with a strand of pearls, and her long platinum-blond hair was pinned up loosely with a tortoise-shell clip. A pair of aviator sunglasses shielded her eyes.

"Hi, Nadine! I got you a decaf soy latte with a touch of cinnamon, just the way you like it," the girl announced, handing her one of the cups.

"Oh, marvelous! You are an angel!" Nadine said gratefully as she took a sip.

Emily blinked. Nadine had just gone from scary to sweet in two seconds.

Talk about Jekyll and Hyde, she thought.

The blond slipped off her aviators and turned to Emily. "Hey, Emily! Welcome to Rockabella!"

Emily smiled uncertainly. The girl looked really familiar....

"It's me, Zoe. Zoe Devereaux," the girl reminded her.

Emily nodded. Zoe was a senior at Northside and a cheerleader on the Varsity squad. "Right! I'm sorry! I didn't recognize you out of uniform!"

"That's okay. I don't know if we've actually ever spoken before. Nadine, how's the latte? Did they make it hot enough this time?" Zoe asked.

"It's perfect, Zoe. Just what I needed. Now, could I impose on you to take our new girl to the back room and get her started on the prom dresses?"

"Of course, Nadine." Zoe took Emily by the arm and led her away.

"Thank you, Zoe," Emily said. She wasn't sure if she was thanking Zoe for helping her with the prom dresses, saving her from Nadine, or a little of both.

"No probs! I'm here to assist." Zoe leaned closer to Emily. "So has the boss lady made you pee your pants yet?"

Emily giggled. She peered over her shoulder to make sure Nadine wasn't listening. She wasn't. "Almost! Is she always like that?" she asked Zoe.

"Yes and no. You just have to know how to handle her. I promise to give you some pointers. Have you ever worked retail before?"

Emily shook her head. "Nope. In fact, besides babysitting, this is my first real job."

"Well, you're in luck. I can teach you everything you need to know!"

"Thank you!" Emily repeated. She had a feeling she would be thanking Zoe a lot over the next few weeks.

The back room was small, about the size of Emily's bedroom. Cardboard boxes filled half of it; most of the other half was taken up by clothing racks, an ironing board, a sewing machine, and a couple of garment steamers.

The two girls got busy with the new prom dresses.

Emily pulled a long sapphire-blue gown out of a plastic bag and held it up to the light. "Wow, so this is your last year at Northside. Where are you going to college?" she asked Zoe.

"I'm waiting to hear. April first is the big day when most of the colleges send out their acceptances. My first choice is Tufts. My second choice is Northwestern, and my third choice is NYU," Zoe replied.

"Wow, that's awesome. Good luck!"

"Thanks! You must be getting ready for tryouts, right?"

Emily nodded. "Yeah. Coach Steele just announced the dates. I'm kind of nervous."

"Don't sweat it. You're totally going to make Varsity."

"No, no...I'm not good enough for Varsity yet. Maybe next year. I just want to make the JV squad again."

Zoe's brown eyes widened. "What? You're kidding, right? You're definitely good enough for Varsity! I've seen you at the games. Your top skills are killer!"

Emily beamed. "Really? Thanks! That's so nice of you to say. There's no way I could go for Varsity, though. I'd have to learn how to do a standing back tuck or a standing back handspring tuck ASAP. And a round-off, back handspring, tuck, too. It's impossible."

Zoe put her hands on Emily's shoulders. "Girl, please. Nothing is impossible. Let me help you nail those moves. I know you can do this."

"Really?" Emily stared at Zoe. "Why do you want to help me? You barely even know me."

"Because I'm awesome?" Zoe joked. "Seriously. Let me do this for you. Someone helped me make the Varsity squad three years ago, and I want to pass on the good karma. What do you say?"

Emily hesitated. This was a big decision. "I'll think about it, okay? I promise I'll let you know really soon."

"No, not really soon. *Tonight.* Because if you want to do this, we're going to start practicing tomorrow," Zoe told her firmly.

Tomorrow? Emily tried to hide her surprise. This girl was serious!

The question was: Did Emily really want to go for Varsity?

Because she could think of one person who might not be happy if she did.

CHAPTER 4

Kate made her way down the hallway in the Foreign Language wing of Northside High. Her first class wasn't for another fifteen minutes, but she wanted time at her locker to organize her books and papers. It was a routine she'd gotten into on Monday mornings. It was nice to start the week on an organized note.

Her Monday schedule was a tough one, especially since she had three honors classes, including Mrs. Lawrence's English Lit class. Fortunately, English was one of her favorite subjects. She really liked the novel they were studying now, *Frankenstein* by Mary Wollstonecraft Shelley.

Growing up, she'd thought that Frankenstein was a cartoon monster. Now, she knew it was the name of the mad-scientist doctor who'd created the monster. Kate found the book's theme—people trying to achieve things beyond their abilities—really fascinating.

"Kate! Wait up!"

Kate turned to see Emily speed walking toward her, a large iced coffee in hand.

"Hi, Emily. How was your weekend?" Kate called out.

"Oh, busy! Busy, busy, busy!" Emily took a long sip of her drink and regarded Kate with a wide-eyed expression. She was often like this in the morning, especially when she'd had too much caffeine. "I started my new job on Saturday. At Rockabella. Did I mention that my boss may be part werewolf? Or barracuda? Or whatever? Bottom line, she's a nightmare!"

Kate giggled. "I'm sorry. How often are you working there?"

"Just Saturdays. I'm hoping I can last until summer. I want to save up enough money to buy a new Chad. I am so done with this one." Emily held up her phone, which was purple and covered with faded heart stickers.

"Aww, poor Chad. Maybe you could donate him."

"I hadn't thought of that. Great idea!" Emily took another long sip. "Anyway, that was Saturday. Yesterday, I was with Zoe most of the day. My quads feel like they've been stomped on by a herd of elephants, then run through a blender!"

"*Eww*. Wait, Zoe who?"

"You know. Zoe Devereaux from the Varsity squad. She works at Rockabella, too. She offered to help me with my round-off, back handspring, tuck and other stuff for try-outs. Did I mention that she has this mysterious, magical way of making Nadine act like a nice person? It's weird."

Kate frowned. "Back up. Why are you working on a round-off, back handspring, tuck for tryouts? You don't need to throw one for JV, right?"

Emily hesitated. "Yeah. So the thing is, I've decided to go for Varsity, after all. Zoe convinced me that I have the skills. She's super-sweet. She's like the big sister I always wanted!"

"Oh!" Kate tried to process this. "Wow, good for you! What did Chloe say when you told her?"

"About Zoe being my new big sister?"

"No, about you going for Varsity."

"She . . . uh . . . that is, I haven't told her yet."

"Why not?"

"I don't know. Well, that's not true, I *do* know. Chloe can be a wee bit competitive. Okay, a *lot* competitive. She and Leila have, like, this contest going about which one of them will make Varsity." Emily added, "I overheard Coach

Steele say at practice last Thursday that there are twenty-two spots for Varsity and twenty-two spots for JV next year, *max*. It's crazy, but there are only two Varsity cheerleaders graduating this year. Zoe said the other twenty are definitely trying out for Varsity again. If they all make it, which they probably will, that means—"

"—there are only two possible openings on the Varsity squad," Kate finished.

"Yes! Anyway, so if Chloe, Leila, and I are trying for those two openings, that means one of us definitely *won't* get it."

"Yikes!"

"Exactly. Yikes!"

"What's wrong, you guys?" Chloe fell in step beside them, looking crisp in a pleated plaid skirt and white sweater set. Devin was with her, more casual in faded jeans and a purple henley.

Emily plastered a huge smile on her face. "Oh! Hi, Chloe! Hi, Devin! Kate and I were—um—just talking about global warming!"

"You were?" Chloe asked.

"Uh-huh," Emily fibbed. "It's a really serious problem, and we should all do something about it!"

Kate gave Emily a warning look. She was a big believer in telling the truth. Emily had to come clean with Chloe as soon as possible. Otherwise, Chloe might find out from someone else and get really mad at Emily for keeping a secret from her.

"So you guys? I'm going over to Synergy Gymnastics after school to work on my tumbling for tryouts," Devin announced. "They have open gym on Mondays. It's only five dollars. Does anyone want to come with me?"

"Love to, but there's a spring dance committee meeting that Emily and I have to go to," Chloe replied. "We're working on music, and they want to hear our ideas. We decided to go for a band rather than a DJ. And now we just have to pick one. Right, Em?"

"Uh-huh." Emily nodded distractedly.

"I wish I could go with you, Devin. But I have my first tutoring session," Kate said.

Chloe raised her eyebrows. "Why do you need tutoring, Kate? You're, like, the smartest person in the universe."

Kate grinned. "Hardly! But thanks. It's a new peer-tutoring program that Mr. Alonso started. I'll be tutoring another student. I thought it would be good for me to do some volunteer work."

"But we already do volunteer work as part of the JV squad," Devin said. "Plus, you and Chloe help out at Hearts Heal on weekends, right?"

"Yeah, but I wanted to do more. Anyway, I'm meeting the student after school today. I'm not sure who it'll be. Mr. Alonso will be there to introduce us," Kate explained.

"Maybe, if you're lucky, it'll be your BF, Adam," Emily said with a sly smile. "You can hold hands under the table while you teach him all about similes and megaphones."

"*Metaphors*," Kate corrected her with a laugh. "And I'm sure it's not Adam. He would have told me."

"You two are *such* a cute couple," Emily remarked.

"Stop," Kate said, blushing. But she didn't correct Emily this time.

✳

After school, Kate and Adam lingered outside Mr. Alonso's classroom. They leaned against the lockers and gazed into each other's eyes, their fingertips brushing lightly.

"Why can't you go for a walk with me? It's really nice out," Adam said, weaving his fingers through hers. He'd started letting his black hair grow longer so that it curled softly over his neck. He wore faded jeans and a gray T-shirt that read ZENO MOVES ME. Kate wasn't positive, but she thought it was a reference to the Greek philosopher Zeno, who'd tried to prove that motion was impossible.

"I wish I could. But I have this tutoring thing now," Kate explained patiently.

"Cancel. Tell Mr. A. you have an emergency," Adam joked.

Kate laughed. "You mean like an 'I have to go for a walk with my boyfriend' emergency? I'm sure he'd love that."

Adam grinned. "Ah, well. I tried. So what's the subject?"

"I'm not sure. I think English? Or maybe Creative Writing? Mr. Alonso didn't give me all the details."

"Text me as soon as you're done. If it's not too late, maybe we can still go on that walk."

"It's a deal. Or you could come over for dinner. Dad and Barbara are making pizza tonight. Sasha's been asking about you. And Garrett and Jack want to show you their new Matchbox cars." Two-year-old Sasha was Kate's little sister; Garrett and Jack, who were six and four, were her stepbrothers.

"How can I say no to pizza and Matchbox cars—and you?" Adam leaned over and kissed her. "Okay, Cheer Girl. Go tutor! Spread your genius around the world! Text me later!" With that, he turned and disappeared down the hall.

Kate stood there for a second, her lips still tingling from Adam's kiss. She liked him so much. More than any other boy she had ever known. They'd started out as friends last September, and then their friendship had slowly, gradually blossomed into more.

There had been obstacles along the way. Kate wasn't the most confident girl. It had taken her a long time to believe that a boy could like her back, especially a cute, smart, amazing boy like Adam, who also happened to be a junior.

For another thing, Adam's friends had been really rude to her. Especially one friend, Willow, who had acted like *she* was Adam's girlfriend. Apparently, she'd had a secret crush on Adam, and she hadn't been happy about Kate hanging around. She'd almost managed to break up Kate and Adam's relationship—but in the end, Adam had gotten Willow to confess the truth about her weird, manipulative behavior, and he and Kate had made up.

Kate was suddenly aware of people walking past her into Mr. Alonso's classroom. She peeked at her watch. She didn't want to be late.

She adjusted her backpack and headed inside. Mr. Alonso was talking to a couple of sophomore boys.

"Oh, hello, Kate. Thanks for coming!" Mr. Alonso called out to her. "Your student isn't here yet. I'm just filling in these gentlemen on the program details, and then I'll get to you. Have a seat."

Kate nodded and sat down at a nearby desk.

Mr. Alonso was one of the history teachers at Northside. He was in charge of the peer-tutoring program and the mock trial team, too. Maps of various countries covered the walls of his classroom. Posters of Martin Luther King Jr. and Gandhi hung over his desk.

A girl strolled into the room, texting intently on her phone. Kate bit back her surprise. It was Willow Zelinski—the person who'd almost destroyed Adam and Kate's relationship.

Willow wore a short pleated skirt, tight-fitting purple

top, and lace-up boots. With her waist-length auburn hair and chunky black glasses, she looked geeky and gorgeous at the same time.

Willow glanced at Kate but didn't acknowledge her as she took an empty seat across the room, still texting. Kate wondered what she was doing here. She knew Willow was super-smart. *I guess she's tutoring someone, too,* Kate thought.

"Please put your phone away, Willow. You know that's against the rules," Mr. Alonso called out.

Willow rolled her eyes and tucked her phone into her backpack.

Mr. Alonso got up and walked over to where Kate was sitting. He gestured for Willow to join him. Willow sighed dramatically and got up.

"Willow, meet Kate MacDonald. Kate, meet Willow Zelinski," Mr. Alonso said. "Kate is a freshman. Willow is a junior. Kate, Willow needs some assistance with her Creative Writing class."

Kate and Willow stared at each other. Willow looked as horrified as Kate felt.

"But—" Willow began.

"But—" Kate began at the same time.

Mr. Alonso frowned. "Is there a problem, ladies?"

Yes! Kate wanted to shout.

How could she and Willow possibly work together?

CHAPTER 5

"Soooo. My little sister is a big-deal cheerleader," Sage Isle said as she made a left turn onto Hawthorn Street. "I never thought I'd see the day!"

Devin grinned. "Um, thanks?"

"You're welcome. Makes sense, though, since you worship the ground I walk on and want to copy everything I do," Sage joked.

"Yeah, that's why I decided to become a cheerleader."

"Seriously, though. I'm proud of you. I had coffee with Coach Steele yesterday, and she said you've been a great cocaptain this year."

"She did?"

"She did. She said that you and your cocaptain—Courtney?"

"Chloe."

"That you and Chloe work together really well, and that you complement each other's leadership skills. She said you guys did an awesome job preparing the squad for Nationals."

"Huh." Devin was surprised to hear this. Coach Steele, while generally positive and supportive, didn't give compliments easily.

Devin was on her way to Synergy Gymnastics to take advantage of their open gym time. Sage, who was home for spring break, had offered to drive her, since the gym was a long bus ride away. Their mom, Linda, was working the late shift in the PICU at Sunny Valley County Hospital.

Sage glanced in the rearview mirror and smoothed back her long, curly red hair. For some reason, it always looked neater and less frizzy than Devin's. It was so unfair. "How's Mom doing these days?" Sage asked.

"Oh, you know. She gets super-stressed at work. And she hasn't been the same since she found out Dad's got a new girlfriend," Devin replied.

"Yeah. It's been less than a year since they split up. I'm sure she's not happy."

"She's not."

"What about you? What's going on with you and Josh?"

"We...um...we split up, too. At the Valentine's Day dance. It was too hard to make the long-distance thing work." Devin gazed out the window, remembering how Josh had come all the way down to surprise her at the dance—only to find her slow-dancing with Mateo. "He just changed his profile picture on Facebook. It's a photo of him hiking in Lake Tahoe with some girl," she added.

"Oooh, jealous?"

"Nah. Well, maybe a little." Devin laughed. She could never hide anything from her big sister. "I kind of like this other boy now. At my school. His name's Mateo Torres. He's on the JV basketball team—oh, and his brother Leo's a sophomore at USC."

"Leo Torres? No way! I know him."

"You do?"

"Yeah. He used to date a friend of mine there. He's hella smart."

"So is Mateo."

"Aw. My little sis is a big-deal cheerleader *and* she has a new boyfriend. Sounds like life in Sunny Valley is pretty sunny."

"Mateo isn't my—"

"Here we are!" Sage trilled as she turned into a parking lot. "I noticed a cute little café around the corner. I'm going to grab a latte and catch up on my e-mail and stuff. Text me when you're ready to go, okay?"

"Sounds good. Thanks for the ride."

"Yeah, you owe me, sis."

Devin grabbed her duffel bag, exited Sage's ancient VW, and headed into Synergy Gymnastics. In the lobby, she signed in at the front desk and gave the woman five dollars for the open gym fee.

Inside the gym, a dozen girls and guys took turns running tumbling passes on the mats while staff spotters stood by. Devin set her bag down on a bench, pulled off her sneakers, and began doing hamstring stretches on the floor.

As Devin reached for her toes, she watched a guy run across the gym and throw a punch front through to a round-off, back handspring, full. She thought about all the years she'd spent on the Rocket Gymnastics team back in Spring Park. She really, really liked cheerleading and would never consider giving it up. But gymnastics was her first love, and she missed it—a *lot*. Even now, as she watched the guy nail his landing, she felt a vicarious thrill. Now *that* was a landing! Her muscles reacted instinctively, and her arms started to lift in a V.

She willed them to stay in her lap and smiled to herself, embarrassed. She wasn't here to go down memory lane. She was here to practice her tumbling for cheerleading tryouts.

"Well, well!"

A tall, lanky brunette strode up to her, dressed in a white T-shirt and shorts. It was Leila Savett. "Devin Isle! What are you doing here?" she trilled. Her voice was friendly, but it had an edge to it, too.

Devin stood up and reached behind to grab her right foot in a quadriceps stretch. "Hey, Leila. I'm here to practice my tumbling for tryouts. What about you?"

"Me too."

Leila pulled her shiny black hair up in a scrunchie and regarded Devin with her ice-blue eyes. "Soooo. I've been meaning to ask. Why aren't you trying out for Varsity? You know how to do most of the requirements already. Not to mention, you're a way better cheerleader than Chloe Davis," she said sweetly.

Devin frowned. She wasn't falling for Leila's old divide-and-conquer trick. She'd had enough of that last autumn when Leila had tried to make Devin and Chloe turn against each other.

"Chloe's one of the best cheerleaders I've ever met," Devin stated. "As for me...I'm happy on the JV squad. I'll be honored if I'm picked to be on the squad again. Besides, I can always try out for Varsity next year."

"Whatevs. But I think you're making a big mistake. You and I would be an awesome duo on the Varsity squad." Leila gave a little wave. "Later!"

She strolled over to the corner of the gym and waited in line behind a couple of girls. When it was her turn, she sprinted across the floor and launched into a round-off, back handspring, tuck. Her movements were clean, although she couldn't stick her landing. Her arms flailed, and she wobbled on her feet. As she straightened herself, her expression was angry, as though she were looking for someone to blame for her less-than-perfect performance.

Devin finished stretching and joined the line. She waited for two people in front of her to complete their passes. When it was her turn, she threw a warm-up pass. And then another.

After a while, she was ready to try a round-off, back handspring, full.

She closed her eyes briefly and visualized herself doing it perfectly. She imagined leaning back during the rebound and pushing her hips forward. She pictured landing on the balls of her feet.

Her eyes snapped open. She took off running. When she hit the middle of the floor, her instincts and muscle memory took over. She wasn't performing the round-off, back handspring, full. She *was* the round-off, back handspring, full.

Stick the landing. Arms up!

A bead of sweat ran down her forehead. She swiped her hand across her face and jogged back to the end of the line. Adrenaline coursed through her veins. That had felt good. *Really* good.

All of a sudden, she was aware of clapping from the sidelines. A girl in a leotard gave her a thumbs-up. A boy wearing the Breckenridge High colors whistled.

Behind them, an older man and a woman in matching powder-blue tracksuits stared at Devin and whispered to each other.

Wow, I've got an audience, Devin thought.

She continued running passes for the next hour, taking almost no breaks. She was in the zone, and she didn't want to stop.

At one point, the man and the woman in the tracksuits came up to her. "Excuse me," the man said, extending his hand. "I'm Joe Logan. This is my wife, Wendy. We coach the Synergy girls' gymnastics teams."

"Oh! Hi!" Devin shook their hands. "I'm Devin Isle."

"It's very nice to meet you, Devin," Mrs. Logan said pleasantly. "We were just wondering—which club are you with?"

"I'm not. I mean, I used to be, when I lived in Spring Park. That's near San Francisco. I belonged to the Rocket Gymnastics Club, Level 8. But I'm a cheerleader now. I'm on the JV squad at Northside High."

"Why'd you switch?" Mr. Logan asked curiously.

"I—well, it's a long story. When my mom and I moved here last September, Coach Steele asked me to join the squad. She knew our family from Spring Park because she used to coach my big sister, Sage. It meant a lot to my mom, so I said yes."

"Of course. That's totally understandable," Mrs. Logan agreed.

Mr. Logan nodded. "Absolutely. So, Devin, are you as comfortable on the vault, beam, and bars as you are on the floor?"

"Yes! I actually really miss the vault, beam, and bars," Devin confessed with a smile.

The Logans exchanged a look.

"Well, Devin! You sound like our kind of gymnast," Mr. Logan said after a moment. "In fact, we're preparing for the Southern California Superstars Gymnastics Tournament right now. It's a stepping stone to the Junior Olympics. We could sure use someone with your amazing skills."

"I'm sorry...*what?*" Devin wasn't sure she was hearing correctly.

Mrs. Logan laughed. "I know, I know. You're asking yourself, who are these people, and why are they trying to recruit me? But we know exceptional talent when we see it. You have a real future as a gymnast. A *competitive* gymnast. But I'm sure you know that already."

Devin didn't know that at all, though being an Olympic gymnast had once been her greatest dream. She stared at the Logans, unsure of what to say.

"Please just think about it," Mr. Logan said. "Here's our card. Don't hesitate to call if you have any questions. Your mom is also welcome to call us, anytime. We'd love to meet with the two of you at your convenience. The Level 8 team practices here Tuesdays through Fridays after school from four to six, plus Saturdays from nine to eleven. The tournament is in May."

"Um, thanks." Devin took the card from him and slipped it into her shorts pocket.

As Devin started to say good-bye to the Logans, she noticed someone standing nearby, obviously eavesdropping.

It was Leila.

CHAPTER 6

Emily sat on the bleachers, watching intently as the Northside Varsity cheerleaders practiced their stunts. They were good. *Really* good. Emily was especially entranced by a stunt group that was executing a ground-up liberty, which wasn't even the hardest stunt that they could perform. Zoe had volunteered to help coach the group today. Like Emily, Zoe was a top. As the bases lifted her to the pinnacle, Zoe raised her arms straight up and touched her right foot to her left knee. Her smile was so big and radiant as she looked out at the bleachers that it made Emily smile back automatically in response.

Zoe was the best kind of cheerleader—someone who *inspired*.

"Let's try that again," Zoe called out to the other girls in her group as she was lowered to the ground. "This time, Danielle, you take my place. Bases, don't forget to wait a split second during the lift so Danielle has time to get her hips above her knee."

Emily grabbed her notebook and spread it out on her lap. It was a new one, and she'd labeled it VARSITY TRY-OUT TIPS. She'd been keeping careful notes on everything Zoe had taught her so far, including the secret to throwing a standing tuck and some home exercises for general conditioning.

Had it only been three days since Emily had first spoken to Zoe, at Rockabella? Emily felt so lucky. In that short amount of time, Zoe had shown her the ropes at the store, run interference with Nadine, convinced her to try out for Varsity, *and* given her a personal coaching session. Earlier today, she'd found Emily in study hall and suggested that she stop by the Varsity practice to pick up additional pointers.

Chad began buzzing. "Oh no!" Emily muttered under her breath. She'd forgotten to turn it off—and Coach Steele was sitting less than ten feet away!

Emily reached into her pocket and fumbled around

for the Off button. "Come on, come on, come on," she whispered.

Chad went silent just as Coach Steele glanced over her shoulder suspiciously. She caught Emily's eye and nodded a greeting. Emily nodded back. *Whew.*

A man strode into the gym and signaled for Coach Steele's attention. She stood up and walked in his direction.

Emily frowned. He looked familiar. He had curly gray-black hair, an athletic build, and a confident expression that suggested that he felt at home in the Northside gym. No, more than that—like he *owned* it. He wore a teal polo shirt, khakis, and white leather sneakers.

Coach Steele joined him, and they exchanged a few words. The coach's demeanor was pleasant and polite, but her shoulders were raised and tense.

Who is that guy? Emily wondered.

The man said something else to Coach Steele. Emily wished she were close enough to eavesdrop. Was he one of the judges? But that didn't make sense. The identity of the judges was usually a big secret until the actual tryout date.

Emily returned her attention to the Varsity girls and scribbled more notes in her notebook. After a while, the cheerleaders took a break. Zoe trotted over to where Emily sat.

"How's it going?" Zoe asked, wiping her brow with a towel. "Are you learning lots and lots?"

"Yes! Thanks so much for suggesting that I be here," Emily replied.

"You should come to these practices as much as you can. You know, it's important to perfect your technique in the basics and skills you already know," Zoe remarked.

"Definitely," Emily agreed.

"Were you watching Danielle's group's stunt? The ground-up liberty? When your group does it, make sure you rise to a standing position really quickly."

Emily wrote this down in her notebook. She, Chloe, Kate, and Devin had attempted the stunt last Thursday—and failed. "Uh-huh."

Zoe was only one of two seniors on the Varsity squad. The other was a girl named Mallory Stein, who was their captain. The remaining twenty girls consisted of sixteen juniors and four sophomores. Zoe and Mallory didn't have to be at the practices anymore, now that basketball season was over and they were so close to graduating. But they'd volunteered to be at some of the sessions to help prepare their squad mates for tryouts. They had also volunteered to teach everyone the tryout dance and cheer at the April clinics.

"Hey, Zoe?" Emily pointed to the gray-haired man. "See that guy talking to Coach Steele? Who is he?"

Zoe followed Emily's gaze. "That's Mr. Piretti. He's the assistant coach for the Varsity squad at Breckenridge."

"Oh!" Breckenridge was one of Northside's biggest rivals. The school was so rich that there was a head coach *and* an assistant coach for the Varsity squad. Plus a head coach and an assistant coach for JV, too. "What's he doing here?"

Zoe lowered her voice. "Can you keep a secret?"

"Yes!" Emily made a zipping motion across her mouth.

"Okay, so...right now, Coach Steele is in charge of the Varsity *and* JV cheerleaders, right? But the Northside administration suddenly decided that it had more money in the budget for the cheer program. Maybe it's because you guys came in fifth at Nationals, I don't know. Anyway, they're hiring a new coach so that Coach Steele doesn't have to do both. She's a candidate for the Varsity job. So is Mr. Piretti. He's a good friend of Principal Cilento."

"Wait, what? If Coach Steele gets the job, does that mean she won't be the JV coach anymore?"

"Exactly."

"How do you know all this?" Emily asked Zoe curiously.

"I know everything, my little apprentice. Oh, looks like break is over." Zoe took a swig from her water bottle and jumped to her feet. "Don't forget, this stuff is top secret. You can't tell any of your friends, okay?"

"I won't."

"Oh, and tonight, I'm going to e-mail you a link to something called Varsity TV. I want you to watch the cheerleading videos. We're talking *the* most crisp and crystal-clear motions you've ever laid eyes on. They're so good, they'll make you cry. Study them carefully, okay? No detail is too small if you're going to ace the tryouts."

"Okay."

Emily observed the rest of the practice, deep in thought. She couldn't imagine Meg Steele *not* coaching the JV squad. Of course, she deserved to be the Varsity coach, if that was what she wanted. She would be able to devote more time to the one squad. And if Emily made Varsity, she would continue to be under Coach Steele's leadership.

Still, this was big news. Emily was dying to tell Chloe, Kate, and Devin. She dug through her pocket, searching for Chad.

But she couldn't. She'd promised Zoe.

At five o'clock, practice began wrapping up. Emily waved good-bye to Zoe and slipped out the double doors. She knew that her brother Chris would be waiting in the parking lot to give her a ride home.

Emily ran into Chloe just outside the gym.

"Hey, Chlo! Love to chat, but I've gotta run," Emily said with a nervous smile. "Text me later?" She was bursting with the hot gossip about Coach Steele, and she was afraid she might let it slip out.

Chloe glared at her. "Where were you?" she demanded.

Emily stopped in her tracks. "What? Why?"

"You missed the spring dance committee meeting. You were supposed to be there. I was only there because you told me we had to go."

Emily froze. *Oops.* She'd totally forgotten about the meeting. "Oh, *that*," she finally managed.

"Yes, *that*. How can you talk me into helping you and then bail?"

"I'm really sorry," Emily murmured.

"I texted you like five hundred times. Why didn't you answer?"

Emily pulled Chad out of her pocket and turned it on. A dozen texts popped up, all from Chloe:

Meeting is starting soon.
I'm here. Where r u?
Meeting started.
Seriously where are you?????
EMILY????????????

And so on.

"I...um...my phone was turned off," Emily admitted.

Chloe put her hands on her hips. "Why?"

"Because...um...I was in the gym. Watching the Varsity practice."

"I don't get it. What were you doing there?" Chloe asked, confused.

"I—um—" Emily stared down at her feet. "I decided to try out for Varsity," she said in a voice barely above a whisper.

Chloe gasped. "Excuse me? *What?*"

"I decided to try out for Varsity. I'm sorry, I was going to tell you."

"Really? When?"

"Soon. Right now. I don't know." Emily shrugged.

"When did you decide this?"

"On Saturday."

"Why didn't you tell me then?" Chloe asked.

"Because..." Emily hesitated. "Because I was afraid you'd be mad at me. And see, I was right." She crossed her arms over her chest defensively.

"I'm not mad because you're trying out. I'm mad because you lied to me," Chloe huffed.

"I didn't lie, I just didn't tell you right away. There's a difference."

"No, there isn't!"

"Yes, there is!"

Chloe shook her head. "I can't talk to you," she said, then turned and stormed off.

Emily watched her friend go, her eyes stinging with tears. Why was Chloe so angry with her? More important, how was she going to fix this?

CHAPTER 7

Chloe flopped down on her bed with its plush indigo quilt and gazed out the French doors. Her dog, Valentine, jumped up and began licking her face.

"Not now," Chloe said, pushing the little white bichon frise away. Valentine whimpered and curled up in an unhappy ball at Chloe's feet.

Chloe was in a bad mood. No, not a bad mood—a horrible mood. But why? So Emily had decided to try out for Varsity. So what? Why should Chloe care either way?

She grabbed her teddy bear, Pom, and hugged him to her chest. He wore a blue-and-white cheerleader uniform and held tiny poms.

The problem was that Emily had kept the information from Chloe. Emily had done the same thing back in January, when she'd skipped a cheer practice to attend a meeting with Rampage Records in Los Angeles. She'd told Chloe, Kate, Coach Steele, and the rest of the squad that she had the flu—everyone but Devin, whom she'd decided to confide in for some mysterious reason.

Chloe had thought that was the last of Emily's secrets and lies.

Why was it happening again?

On an impulse, she picked up her phone and dialed Kate's number. She needed to vent to someone.

Kate answered on the first ring. "Hi, Chloe! How are you? I thought you were at the spring dance meeting with Emily," she said.

"*I* was. Emily wasn't. The meeting's over now."

"Oh. How was it?"

"I gave the committee a list of bands that Emily and I came up with," Chloe explained quickly. "Then they reported on their agenda items, like flyers and decorations and stuff. But that's not why I'm calling. *Guess what?*"

"What?"

"Emily's trying out for Varsity!" Chloe announced.

There was a long silence.

"Kate? Are you there?"

"I'm here. I—um—knew that already."

Chloe wasn't sure she'd heard Kate right. "I'm sorry, *what?*"

"Emily mentioned it to me this morning. At school. I guess Zoe Devereaux convinced her to go for Varsity. They work together at Rockabella. Zoe's one of the two senior cheerleaders who's graduating this year."

"I know who Zoe is. Why would Emily tell you and not me?"

There was another silence.

"Kate?" Chloe prompted.

"I think Emily was afraid you'd be mad at her," Kate said finally. "You know, because the competition's so fierce for Varsity, and you and Leila are already trying out for what may end up being just two open spots."

"Why would I be mad?" Chloe snapped, more loudly than she'd intended. Valentine began barking.

Kate laughed uncomfortably. "You sound pretty mad right now."

"Well, I'm not!" Chloe took a deep breath and reached over to pet Valentine. They both needed to calm down. "Okay, maybe I am. But I'm not mad because Emily's going for Varsity. I'm mad because she didn't tell me."

"I know, I know. You should just talk to her."

"Yeah. Maybe. I don't know."

Chloe heard a crashing sound on the other end of the phone, followed by high-pitched screams. "Sorry. My little sister just knocked down the boys' LEGO tower. They've spent a whole week building it," Kate explained.

"Uh-oh."

"I'd better go. Adam's coming over for dinner. By the way, did I tell you who I'm tutoring?"

"Who?"

"Willow!"

Chloe gasped. "That girl who lied and said Adam was cheating on you with her?"

"The same! I have to help her with her poems and short stories for her Creative Writing class."

"That's awful! Can you get out of it?"

Kate sighed. "No. We're meeting on Wednesday after school to go over her new assignment."

"Aw. I'm sorry. Let me know if there's anything I can do."

"Thanks. Hey, are you free this Sunday? Dad and Barbara are taking us to the beach. You should come with. It sounds like you could use some chill time."

"I wish! But I'm spending every spare minute prepping for tryouts. I'm on a super-strict schedule. I'll be able to hang out after April ninth, though."

"Okay. But don't push yourself too hard, all right?"

"I won't. Thanks, Kate. Talk to you later."

Just as Chloe hung up, her phone buzzed with a text. It was from her mother:

Home 20 min with dinner. Plz set table.

Whatever, Chloe thought.

Downstairs, Chloe found Jake and Clementine in the living room, sprawled on the couch and watching TV on the giant plasma screen. The twins were home for spring break. Their father sat nearby, scrolling through his phone and jotting down notes on a legal pad.

"Yo, Munchkin!" Jake called out. He'd always had various nicknames for Chloe, like Munchkin, Peanut, Shrimp, and Mini-Davis. Which was totally unfair, since Chloe wasn't *that* short—just shorter than him. These days, he towered at six feet three. "You wanna make me some nachos?"

"Make your own nachos, lazy," Clem chided him. With her long strawberry-blond hair and hazel eyes, she looked like an older version of Chloe.

"Mom texted. She's bringing home dinner," Chloe announced. "She said to set the table. Dad, did you get my message?"

"Hmm? What message, honey?" Mr. Davis barely glanced up from his phone.

"My message about the binder for biology. You were supposed to pick one up for me at Office World. I need it for tomorrow's lab."

"What? No, I'm sorry, I forgot. Can you text your mother? Maybe she can swing by Office World on her way home."

"What's she bringing for dinner?" Jake asked. He took off his sports socks, wadded them into a ball, and tossed them into a wastebasket across the room. "Three-point shot!" he hollered.

"She didn't say. Maybe Chinese or Thai?" Chloe guessed. Mr. and Mrs. Davis were both so busy with their jobs that the family had takeout three or four nights a week.

Chloe walked over to the dining room area, which opened onto the living room and kitchen. She grabbed a pile of dark purple place mats and matching cloth napkins from the buffet drawer.

Clem got up to join her. "So, Chlo! Mom told us the big news."

"What big news?"

"That you're trying out for Varsity."

Chloe handed the napkins to her sister. "Yeah. The competition's going to be intense, though."

"You know the secret to nailing tryouts, Mini-Davis?" Jake piped up from the couch. "Stand out! Everyone's going to know how to throw a tuck. Have the biggest smile and the sharpest motions. Sure, you have to be a team player. But at the same time, you have to show the judges that you're special, that you've got star quality."

"Huh," Chloe said. She hadn't thought of it quite that way.

"Are you sure you want to do this, Chloe?" Clem asked her quietly. "You have a leadership role on the JV squad. The other girls look up to you. Don't you want to carry that through for another year, regardless of whether you're captain again?"

59

"That's a good point." Chloe hadn't considered this, either.

"It wouldn't hurt to have another year on JV. You can really hone your skills that way," Clem went on. "Anyway, it's something to think about. Why don't you get the plates and silverware, and I'll fill up the water glasses?"

Chloe nodded slowly. She'd had no idea that tryouts would be so complicated—and she wasn't referring to the tumbling and stunts.

After dinner, Chloe helped clear the dishes, then decided to head up to her room instead of watching a movie with the rest of the family. She had some algebra homework to finish.

As she passed through the foyer, she glanced toward the big picture window—and saw a strange sight. Curious, she moved closer and peered out. In the waning light, she could see two figures across the street. They were playing leapfrog in the grass.

No, they weren't playing leapfrog. They were trying to build a two-person pyramid—and failing horribly.

It was Jasmyn and her friend Beatrice.

Chloe shook her head quickly and started for the stairs. *Don't get involved*, she told herself.

But she couldn't help it. The girls were so young and inexperienced, just like she used to be.

Chloe turned around, opened the door, and headed outside. *Don't get involved*, she kept telling herself as she crossed the street.

Jasmyn and Beatrice caught sight of her. They scrambled to their feet.

"Hi, Chloe!" Jasmyn called out eagerly. "Did you see us? Did you see us?"

Beatrice smiled and waved.

"Yup, I saw you," Chloe replied.

"And?" Jasmyn prompted.

"First of all, never, ever try to stunt without a spotter. It's not safe," Chloe told them sternly.

The girls just stared at her.

"I'll help you, okay? Maybe twice a week after school between now and April. I have cheer practice on Tuesdays and Thursdays, so maybe we can meet on Mondays and Wednesdays. Some weeks, it might be just one day or the other. And no, you can't give me your babysitting money. But you can work hard and listen to everything I say. Is that clear?"

Jasmyn and Beatrice broke into huge smiles.

"Oh, thank you, thank you, thank you!" Jasmyn cried.

"Yes, thank you," Beatrice added.

"Timber! Timber! Timber-Chloe!" Jasmyn yelled, throwing her arms up in an awkward V.

Chloe wondered what she had gotten herself into.

CHAPTER 8

"Yeah, so even though I'm pretty much a genius, my parents are forcing me to do these stupid tutoring sessions," Willow explained to Kate over iced cappuccinos at the Mighty Cup. "I have a four-point-oh average in everything except Creative Writing. But it's not my fault. Mr. Heffernan is boring. His assignments are boring. No wonder I keep getting Cs and Ds on my short stories and poems."

She paused to admire her jet-black nails. "I have no idea why Mr. Alonso matched me up with you. You're only a freshman. How can you possibly help me?" she added snidely.

Kate took a deep breath and counted to ten in her head. She desperately wanted to get up and walk out the door. But she couldn't. She'd signed up to be a peer tutor and she couldn't back out just because her student was her least favorite person at Northside High. Or maybe in the world.

"You said on Monday that you have to write a sonnet for next week," Kate said in a calm, even voice that belied her true feelings. "Have you started working on it yet?"

"Yes. I finished it! You probably don't even know what a sonnet is, do you?"

Kate took another deep breath. "A sonnet is a poem that has fourteen lines and a particular rhyme scheme," she rattled off. "With Shakespearean sonnets, which are also known as English sonnets, the rhyme scheme is A-B-A-B, C-D-C-D, E-F-E-F, and G-G. Those last two 'G' lines are called a couplet. With Petrarchan sonnets, which are also known as Italian sonnets, the rhyme scheme is more complicated." She fixed her gaze on Willow's. "Does that answer your question?"

"Uh—uh—" Willow stammered. "Okay. I guess you know what a sonnet is."

"Do you want to show me what you've written?"

"Yeah, I guess."

Willow reached into her backpack, pulled out a crumpled piece of paper, and slid it across the table to Kate. Kate smoothed out the paper and began reading:

SONNET
By Willow Zelinski

Zombies rule. But vampires are even better.
I wish they really existed, but they
Don't. If they did, I would write them a letter
And tell them what things are like during the day.

My cat's name is Molly, and she likes fish.
I also have a dog that is gold.
If Molly could talk, I think that her wish
Would be to be the only pet in our household.

Why can't they make donuts with two holes instead of one?
Or better yet, three holes or four holes or zero?
Oh, yeah. I think they do make doughnuts with none.
Still, whoever invented the other kinds would be a hero.

I think that's all I have to say for now.
Except maybe that some English teachers look and act
    like cows.

THE END

Kate glanced up. Willow beamed at her. "Well? What do you think? It's brilliant, right?"

"Well…um…it might need a little work," Kate said delicately.

"What are you talking about? Where?"

Kate reread the sonnet quickly. "You've got the A-B-A-B, C-D-C-D, E-F-E-F, G-G rhyme scheme down just fine," she said after a moment. "But your sonnet has to be in iambic pentameter. You need to fix that."

"Iambic *what*?"

"Iambic pentameter. It's the rhythm of the poem, the way you count and accent the syllables. Iambic pentameter means each line of the sonnet should have five words or phrases with two syllables each. Each two-syllable pair should have the accent on the second syllable." Then Kate added, "Like the line from the famous balcony scene in Shakespeare's *Romeo and Juliet*: 'But, soft! What light through yonder window breaks?'" She repeated, emphasizing the accents: "'But, SOFT! What LIGHT through YON-der WIN-dow BREAKS?'"

Willow stared at her.

"Does that make sense? You need to rewrite your lines so they fall in that rhythm," Kate said.

"Why? No one cares if there are five bars or four bars or where the accent falls," Willow complained.

"It matters. Like in cheerleading—our dances are choreographed to a certain rhythm and count, and our cheers are written that way, too. It's how we stay together as a cohesive unit. It also *sounds* good to the audience members' ears because it's steady and punchy," Kate explained.

"Oh." Willow made a face. "Ugh, this is hard! Can we take a break and talk about something else?"

"Like what?"

"Like…uh…well, my little sister's birthday is coming up. A week from Sunday. I'm trying to figure out a present for her. Do you have any ideas? You have a little sister, too, right?"

"Sasha's two. How old is your sister going to be?"

"Eight."

"What kind of stuff does she like?"

"Books. Animals. Oh, yeah, and she wants to be a cheerleader when she's older."

Kate grinned. "Really? That's awesome!"

Willow shrugged. "Hardly. I just don't get the appeal. Why do you people enjoy jumping up and down with poms and screaming 'Go, team!' at the top of your lungs? Or 'Go, team' at the top of your lungs in iambic pentameter?" She cracked up at her own joke.

"Have you ever watched us at a game or a pep rally? There's serious athleticism involved. Not to mention building school spirit and bringing everyone together," Kate pointed out.

"Yeah, whatever. I still think cheerleading is lame." Willow slurped down her drink. "Are you doing it again next year, or have you come to your senses?"

"I'm doing it again next year. If I make the cut, that is. Tryouts are next month."

"Why *wouldn't* you make the cut? You're already on the team or squad or whatever you call it, right?"

"You have to try out every year, even if you're already on the squad. And I'll be competing against a ton of people, including the incoming freshmen."

Willow eyed her with interest. "You know what you need? Some confidence."

"Excuse me?"

"The way you said that stuff just now. 'If I make the cut' and 'I'll be competing against a ton of people.' You sounded whiny and weak, like you don't believe in yourself."

Kate stifled an angry retort. *Whiny and weak?* How dare Willow say that!

Still...

Kate had to admit that Willow had a point. She *didn't* believe in herself. In fact, she'd been thinking lately about how much Chloe, Emily, and Devin were doing to prepare for the upcoming tryouts. Chloe was on a self-imposed, super-disciplined schedule to perfect her skills. Emily had a Varsity cheerleader giving her personal coaching sessions. And Devin was spending Monday nights at a private gym.

Kate, on the other hand, was spending most of her free time with Adam. Sure, she was busy with schoolwork and her various volunteer jobs, too. And she'd made it a point to attend the Tuesday and Thursday cheer practices religiously.

But that wasn't enough. Kate felt uneasy about her cheerleading abilities in general. And her tumbling definitely needed improvement.

Kate didn't want to admit these things to Willow, though. So instead, she said: "Let's get back to work, okay? Mr. Alonso won't be happy if he finds out we spent this whole hour gabbing about cheerleading."

"You are soooo boring," Willow complained.

"And you are soooo going to get a D on this poem if you don't get serious."

Willow rolled her eyes but didn't object.

For the rest of their session, Kate advised Willow on how to solve her iambic pentameter problem. She also explained how to create one cohesive theme rather than a bunch of unrelated ones like vampires, pets, doughnuts, and comparing English teachers to cows.

At five o'clock, they got up to go. "Um, thanks," Willow said, although she didn't exactly sound grateful. "See you next Monday. And before I forget, I have a wee little favor to ask you."

"No, I'm not going to rewrite your sonnet for you."

"It's not that. It's about my sister, Sabrina."

"Oh?"

"I was just thinking. Could you and some of your

friends come to her birthday party and be the entertainment? You know, teach her and the other kids some cheers and stuff?"

Kate blinked, confused. "I thought you said cheerleading is lame."

Willow shrugged and smiled. "It is. But my sister doesn't know any better. And it would be the perfect present for her."

"Uh-huh."

"Well? Will you?"

Kate was about to say no. But she couldn't quite bring herself to do it. Willow *seemed* to be making an effort to get along. Or, more accurately, she wasn't being totally horrible.

Besides, this would be for her little sister, who wanted to be a cheerleader....

"I'll talk to some people and let you know," Kate said finally.

Willow grinned. "Great! I'll tell Sabrina you'll be there!"

This time, Kate did the eye-rolling.

CHAPTER 9

"I'll pick you kids up right here in a couple of hours," Mrs. Torres told Devin and Mateo.

"Thanks, Mom! Sammy, you have fun playing mini golf, okay?" Mateo called out to his little brother.

Sammy waved from the backseat.

Mateo took Devin's elbow and guided her toward the waterfront. It was Friday night, and the boardwalk was full of people strolling, cycling, and Rollerblading. Stars twinkled brightly in the deep blue sky. The salt air mingled with the delicious smells wafting from nearby restaurants.

"I hope you're hungry," Mateo said to Devin.

"I'm starving. Where are we going?"

"To one of my favorite places. It's called the Lobster Claw. My dad used to bring us here for lunch sometimes, on weekends. Afterward, he'd take us to the aquarium."

For a second, a sad expression clouded Mateo's face. The subject of his father had that effect on him sometimes. Mr. and Mrs. Torres had gone through a difficult divorce, just like Devin's parents. In fact, it was one of the things that had drawn her to Mateo. They had a lot of war stories to share.

Then the sadness was gone, and Mateo turned to Devin with a big smile. Devin's heart thumped in her chest. He was crazy-cute and sweet and smart, and she'd had a crush on him for months. She still couldn't believe they were hanging out.

"I'm glad you were free tonight," he said softly.

"Yeah, me too."

"You look really pretty."

Devin blushed. She'd borrowed a sea-green sundress and vintage pink cardigan sweater from Sage. She'd also dug up an old rhinestone barrette to hold back her wild red curls. "Thanks."

"You're welcome."

After a short stroll down the boardwalk, they reached the Lobster Claw, where they managed to get the last available table. The restaurant was a wooden shack that opened up to a spectacular view of the ocean. The walls were painted turquoise, bright yellow, and other tropical colors. The ceilings were strung with hundreds of tiny, twinkling Christmas lights.

Devin thought it was magical—and incredibly romantic. But she didn't say so out loud. She didn't want Mateo to misunderstand or think that she was being presumptuous. She wasn't sure they were on a date tonight, exactly.

"I hope you like this place," Mateo said. "I've never been here for dinner. It's pretty romantic at night, isn't it?" He reached across the table and squeezed her hand.

I guess we're on a date, then, Devin thought happily.

The waiter came by to take their orders. Devin ordered the fish tacos and a root beer. Mateo got the same, and added a side of tortilla chips and guacamole for them to share.

"So how's cheerleading practice going?" Mateo asked Devin when the waiter had brought their drinks and appetizer.

"Good. It's different from before, when we were preparing for Nationals and cheering for the games," Devin replied. "We can kind of do our own thing. You know, practice our skills and do stunts with our groups. Coach Steele pretty much just watches from the sidelines and makes sure we're safe. She gives us tips here and there."

Mateo nodded. "Are you psyched about tryouts?"

Devin hesitated. "Yes. Except—"

"Except what?"

Devin told him about meeting the Logans at Synergy Gymnastics. "They watched me tumbling for a few minutes, and they offered me a spot on their team, just like that," she finished.

Mateo grinned. "That's because you're the best!"

"I'm not! But thanks!"

"So are you going to take them up on their offer?"

"I don't know," Devin confessed. "I can't cheer *and* do club gymnastics. It's against our Cheerleader Contract, and besides, I wouldn't have the time for both."

Mateo nodded. "Yeah, I hear you."

"I'm also rusty on the other elements, like the vault, beam, and bars."

"I'm sure you could get them back really quickly."

Devin reached for a tortilla chip and munched thoughtfully.

"You know what? If I'd met the Logans last September, this would have been a no-brainer," she said after a moment. "I was a gymnast then. I only joined the JV cheer squad because my mom basically forced me. Now...well, I don't know how I feel. I really like being a cheerleader. But I really miss gymnastics, too. I used to dream about becoming a competitive gymnast. If I joined the Logans' team, I could still pursue that goal."

"I totally understand what you're going through," Mateo

said. "I love basketball, and Coach Vettel told me that I had a good chance of making the Varsity team. He said I could play college ball down the line, if I wanted. But I'm interested in other stuff, too. Like diving. In fact, I've been thinking about starting a scuba club at Northside. Plus, my Uncle Eduardo offered me a summer job at his dive shop. That would conflict with basketball camp."

"So you have a tough decision to make, too."

"Yup. I do."

Devin was glad to be able to talk about the Logans' offer with Mateo. She hadn't brought it up with her mom, Sage, Coach Steele, or any of her friends yet. They were all too invested in her being a cheerleader. Mateo, on the other hand, could be neutral and objective. Besides, he really *got* her.

The waiter came by with their fish tacos. Devin picked one up and bit into it. "Oh, my gosh! This is *the* best thing I've ever eaten," she declared.

"Right? Next time, we can try their crab cakes. They're epic. Hey, do you dive?"

Devin's mind was still trying to process the words *next time*. "Seriously? No. I'm afraid of putting my head underwater," she admitted.

Mateo laughed. "I'll teach you, then. That's the only way to overcome your fears—by doing the things you're afraid of."

Like throwing a tuck for the first time, Devin thought. *Like trying a ground-up liberty. Like making new friends. Like breaking up with an old boyfriend. Like exploring a new relationship.*

She silently added: *Like rethinking the whole cheerleading thing and maybe going back to gymnastics.*

❋

When Devin got home that night, she found Sage on the couch channel-surfing and munching on microwave popcorn. Their cat, Emerald, purred contentedly on her lap.

"How was your hot date?" Sage called out.

"It wasn't a date," Devin said quickly, even though it kind of was. "Where's Mom?"

"She called. She had to stay late at the hospital."

"Oh, okay."

"You look nice in my dress. And my sweater. Maybe I should just give them to you."

"Really?" Devin said eagerly.

"Really. But only if you tell me the truth."

"I told you, it wasn't a d—"

"No, I don't mean about your new boyfriend. Something's on your mind. I can tell. You've been acting weird and distracted all week."

Sighing, Devin sat down on the couch beside her sister. Maybe it was time to tell Sage about the Logans, too.

Devin picked up the remote and hit the Mute button. Then she repeated the whole story to her sister.

When she was done, Sage was silent.

"Well?" Devin prompted. "Aren't you going to say something?"

"Yes," Sage said after a moment. "It's great that you're so in demand. And it's great that the Logans appreciate your mad tumbling skills. But you're forgetting a couple of important things."

"Like what?"

"Like, Synergy Gymnastics is a major hike. Mom doesn't have the time to drive you there three, four, five times a week, and once my spring break's over, I won't be around to be your personal chauffeur. Plus, it costs a ton of money. Mom and Dad managed to pay for Rocket Gymnastics when they were together. But now that they're divorced, Mom can barely afford rent or groceries on her nurse's salary. You can't expect her to spring for club fees."

Devin's chest tightened. Sage was right. She was always right.

Sage put her hands on Devin's shoulders. "Be real, sis. There's no way you can join the Synergy team. You'd better say no to the Logans now, before you get your hopes up about being the next Gabby Douglas."

CHAPTER 10

"Zoe is running late this morning," Nadine announced to Emily on Saturday morning. "That means you'll need to unpack all the new shipments yourself. Oh, and you'll need to move these dresses to the sale rack and put fifty-percent-off stickers on the price tags. Perhaps you should start with that before our first customers arrive."

"No problem!" Emily started to turn.

"Did I say I was finished talking?" Nadine said coldly.

Emily whirled back around. "What? No! I'm sorry!"

"Now, about your outfit." Nadine stepped back and looked Emily up and down. "It's slightly better than last week's fashion disaster. But it's still not up to par. *Please* ask Zoe for some clothing advice."

Emily flushed. "I will."

"And about your pedicure. You should be aiming for a neutral, sophisticated look. Bright colors and glitter are neither neutral *nor* sophisticated."

"Yes, of course."

Nadine nodded. "Fine. *Now* I'm finished talking. You may go."

Emily turned away quickly, mostly to keep Nadine from seeing that she was *this close* to crying. Or screaming. Or throwing things. Or all of the above. Nadine had seemed so nice back in January, when she'd donated the outfit for the fashion show fund-raiser. And she positively fawned over Zoe. Why was she so mean to Emily?

Straightening her shoulders, Emily grabbed the box of 50-percent-off stickers from behind the counter. She wasn't sure how much longer she could take this job. By her calculations, she needed to work at least ten Saturdays to make enough money to replace Chad. This was only her second Saturday. How was she going to endure eight more?

For the next half hour, Emily dealt with the sale dresses. She tried to clear her mind and focus on happy thoughts to cheer herself up. Normally, she would text Chloe to vent. But she and Chloe weren't exactly getting along these days. Besides which, Nadine probably had a no-texting-during-work rule. Emily had no interest in finding out what *her* demerit system was like.

Just as she was finishing up with the sale dresses, the front door opened and a customer walked in.

No, not just a customer. A young, male, really *cute* customer.

Emily quickly hid behind a mannequin so she could check him out. He wore a pair of jeans that must have cost as much as the Chad replacement she coveted. His black V-neck sweater complemented his curly reddish-blond hair and made his light blue eyes pop. He looked like a model or a movie star.

He glanced around the store and then at his fancy silver watch. Emily wondered where Nadine was. Maybe in the back room?

Emily checked her face in a nearby mirror. She wore very little makeup, just a touch of pink lip gloss and a hint of peach blush to brighten her olive complexion. She plastered on a big smile, first making sure there was no bagel stuck in her teeth from breakfast, and then strolled over to Mr. Hottie.

"Hi! Is there something I can help you with?" Emily asked, batting her eyelashes. "Are you looking for a present for your girlfriend?" *Say no say no say no*, she prayed.

He shook his head. "No. My girlfriend—I mean, my ex-girlfriend—doesn't like the clothes here. Her style's more East Coast."

"Really?" Emily's mind churned as she tried to analyze his statement. He was unattached. That was a huge plus. But his ex wasn't a Rockabella fan. So what was he doing here?

"I like what you're wearing," he said, pointing to Emily's red sundress and black jean jacket.

Emily beamed. *Take that, Nadine!* "Thanks! I like what you're wearing, too. Are those Q-Brand jeans?" she asked him.

"Yeah, I guess they are. They were a birthday present. I'm Braden, by the way."

"I'm Emily. Emily Arellano."

"You look familiar, Emily Arellano. Do you go to Breckenridge?"

"Definitely not! I go to Northside."

"Why 'definitely not'?"

"They're totally our rivals. I'm a cheerleader."

"Well, I guess that makes us rivals, then. I go to Breckenridge. I'm a senior there."

Emily gasped. Talk about embarrassing. "Oh! I didn't mean—that is—I'm sure Breckenridge is a *great* school!"

"Don't worry about it," Braden said, laughing. "So how long have you been working here?"

"I just started last Saturday." Emily glanced over her shoulder and lowered her voice. "I'm not sure how long I'll last, though. My boss is...um...difficult."

"Really?"

Emily nodded. "Actually, she's a nightmare! But please don't tell her I said that."

"My lips are sealed," Braden promised with a wink.

Emily flushed with pleasure. Her morning had suddenly gone from awful to awesome. Braden was so cool. And gorgeous. And single. Maybe it was time to look *beyond* Northside for boyfriend material....

Nadine emerged from the back room with a clipboard in hand. "Emily, are you finished with the sale rack? Hello, Braden. What are you doing here?"

Hello, Braden?

Emily's gaze bounced between her horrible boss and her future BF. How did they know each other?

Braden leaned over and kissed Nadine on the cheek. "Hey, Mom. My Rover's acting up. Can I borrow your car for a couple of hours to run errands?"

Hey, Mom?

"Fine. Let me get my keys. I just had it washed and waxed, though, so please don't go hot-rodding through mud puddles, all right?"

"Mud puddles? Yeah, there are a lot of those in Sunny Valley. Don't worry about it, Mom," Braden replied.

"If you say so." Nadine went off to find her purse.

Braden turned to Emily with an amused smile. "So. What were we talking about?"

Emily could barely find her voice. "I didn't know she was your mother," she choked out in a miserable whisper.

"It's all right."

"I feel like such a jerk!"

"Seriously, it's fine. I'm not so crazy about her, either."

"You're not?"

"I mean, she's my mom, so I love her and all that. But she can be pretty judgmental."

"I know, right?"

Nadine returned with the keys and handed them to Braden. "Here you go, darling. Emily, why are you standing around? Get to work!" she snapped.

"Emily was helping me pick out a present for Cousin Isabelle's birthday," Braden fibbed.

"Oh! Well, carry on, then." Nadine fluttered her fingers and headed for the back room again.

"Thank you," Emily told Braden gratefully.

"No problem. Why don't you pick out a necklace or scarf or something and tell my mom it's for my cousin? Her birthday's not till June, but Mom won't know the difference. Hang in there. I'll see you around."

"Yes, see you around!"

Braden left. Emily picked up the box of 50-percent-off stickers and returned them to the cash register. She couldn't believe that someone as nice as Braden was related to Nadine. Not just related, but her *son*.

She couldn't wait to tell her friends about him. Would his Breckenridge affiliation be an issue? They might be mad at her for hanging out with "the enemy." He was also a senior, which meant that he was three years older than her. What would her parents think about that?

But maybe she was getting a little ahead of herself. She'd only just met the guy....

❋

Zoe finally showed up at lunchtime. Emily was alone in the store, since Nadine had stepped out to get a salad.

"Zoe! I'm so glad to see you! Where've you been?" Emily demanded.

Zoe took off her sunglasses and tucked them into her purse. "I'm sorry I'm late! I had to watch my little sister this morning because my mom got called into work. She's an ER doctor. What did I miss?"

"Not much. I moved a bunch of dresses to the sale rack and unpacked a ton of boxes. Nadine just went out for lunch. Oh, and I met her son!"

"Braden? Yeah, he's a sweetheart."

"He is, isn't he?" Emily gushed.

Zoe chuckled. "Uh-oh. Someone's got a crush."

"No, I don't! Well, okay, yes, I do."

"Uh-huh. Absolutely no boys until after April ninth, do you hear me? Tryouts have to be your number one priority."

Zoe put her purse behind the counter. "Speaking of which, why weren't you at the Varsity practice on Wednesday?"

"I was *going* to go. But I—um—ran into my friend Chloe after practice on Monday."

"So?"

"So I had to tell her that I'm trying out for Varsity. She got really mad."

"Because...?"

"Because she's trying out for Varsity, too."

Zoe's brown eyes flashed. "You know what, Emily? Having to compete against your friends is a part of life. Especially when you're involved in something as important as cheerleading. Your friend Chloe needs to deal with it. *You* need to deal with it. Growing up is all about tough choices."

"Yeah, I guess you're right," Emily said glumly.

"I'm *totally* right. And don't look so miserable! You and Chloe will work it out. Besides, I have some great news."

Emily perked up. "Really? What?"

"I've got a genius plan that will give you a competitive edge during tryouts!" Zoe announced.

"What kind of genius plan?" Emily asked curiously.

"My neighbor Mrs. Van Dorn is looking for a babysitter for her six-year-old twins. You're going to apply for that job," Zoe explained.

Emily frowned. "I don't get it. How is babysitting for your neighbor going to give me an edge at tryouts?"

"That's the genius part! Mrs. Van Dorn used to be a USC cheerleader, like, a decade ago. I just found out that she's going to be one of the judges at the Northside try-outs. *Your* tryouts. If you can get this babysitting job with her, you'll have an inside advantage on April ninth. Do you understand what I'm saying?"

"Um..." Emily hesitated. "How do you even know that she's going to be one of our judges? Isn't that supposed to be a big secret?"

"Yes. That information's *top* secret. I happened to over-hear Coach Steele and Mr. Piretti discussing it yesterday."

"Oh!"

Zoe pulled her phone out of her pocket. "I can text Mrs. Van Dorn now and suggest that she meet with you ASAP."

Emily turned away and began refolding a pile of sweaters on a shelf. "I'm really, really grateful for your help. But I'm not sure about this plan. It sounds, you know, *illegal* or something," she said after a moment.

Zoe shook her head. "It's totally not! Besides, if you really want to win a spot on the Varsity squad, you have to use every advantage you have. And trust me, babysitting for Mrs. Van Dorn would be a *huge* advantage."

"Yeah, okay."

But Emily had a feeling that Zoe's plan was not okay—not okay at all.

CHAPTER 11

On Saint Patrick's Day, all the JV girls wore green to cheerleading practice. As Chloe prepared to throw a tuck, she smoothed her kelly green T-shirt over her shorts, closed her eyes, and quietly counted: "Five, six, seven, eight…"

Coach Steele stood nearby, her arms at her sides, ready to catch Chloe if necessary. On "one," Chloe opened her eyes, pushed off her toes, and jumped. She reminded herself not to throw her head back and to just go for the height.

Midair, Chloe stretched her arms over her head, still keeping her eyes straight ahead. She lifted her hips and flipped her legs over her shoulders. She caught her knees with her hands as she rotated. Finally, she found the ground and landed cleanly.

"Good! Next time, think about bringing your legs up to your arms rather than your arms down to your legs," Coach Steele advised her. "Make sense?"

Chloe nodded. "Yes! Can I try that again?"

"Actually, why don't you take a break? You've been going nonstop for a while. Besides, I need to give some of the other girls a spot." Coach Steele turned and walked over to where Gemma Moore and her stunt group were practicing their tic-tock.

Chloe grabbed her water bottle, sat down on a bench, and took a long, thirsty gulp of water. She hadn't realized that she'd been practicing so intensely. She was tired, and her muscles felt like Jell-O. She made a mental note to take a long Epsom-salt bath when she got home.

Leila sauntered over and sat down next to her. "Hey, Chloe. I was watching your tuck just now," she remarked casually.

Chloe capped her water bottle and swiped at her mouth with the back of her hand. "Oh?"

"It made me think about that practice last fall. You know, when you tried to throw a tuck and fell on your head."

Chloe's hazel eyes widened. "Excuse me, I did *not* fall

on my head. Coach caught me. Besides, it was my first attempt at a tuck, and—"

"Yeah, yeah. You keep telling yourself that," Leila cut in. "It's like that other time when you thought you could be a top. You tanked your dismount, sprained your ankle, and almost cost our squad the Regionals win. Talk about a colossal fail!"

Chloe's cheeks grew hot. Leila was obviously trying to psych her out.

"It's not working, Leila," Chloe seethed.

"What's not working? I'm just trying to make a point."

"Which is what?"

"Don't pretend to be a better cheerleader than you are. You should stay on the JV squad where you belong." Leila smirked. "Later!"

Chloe watched her former friend walk away and join Marcy Martinez on the mats. Didn't Leila get tired of being so mean all the time? Chloe remembered when Leila used to be a nice person. Now, all she seemed to care about was winning at any cost. There was *healthy* competition and *unhealthy* competition. Leila's behavior definitely fell in the latter category.

Chloe toweled off her face and scanned the gym. Her seventeen squad mates were spread out, some practicing their stunts in groups, others working individually on their motions, jumps, or tumbling. Chloe watched as Devin launched a running pass, finishing with a full. The girl was scary-good.

Emily went next, completing her pass with a tuck. Chloe did a double take. When had Emily learned to throw a tuck? It wasn't perfect; she hadn't achieved enough height, and her landing had been wobbly. But still.

Chloe and Emily hadn't spoken since their fight outside the gym last Monday. It was bad enough that Emily had made the decision to go for Varsity and not tell Chloe. For the past week, Chloe had done everything for their so-called music subcommittee for the spring dance. In fact, she'd spent hours on Sunday afternoon checking out band demos online. That was time she should have spent practicing cheers instead. Chloe had texted Emily to try to split up the task, but Emily had texted back and said she had somewhere she had to be.

Probably working on her tuck with her new friend Zoe, Chloe thought bitterly.

The thing was...Chloe missed Emily. She didn't like not being on speaking terms with her best friend. They were used to sharing everything: what they ate for breakfast, which muscles hurt after practice, which guys they liked and didn't like. Of course, Chloe had Kate to share stuff with. But Kate spent a lot of time with Adam these days. As for Devin, she and Chloe hadn't exactly formed a close friendship outside of their gang of four.

Chloe pouted. The truth was, she felt lonely. All because she and Emily were having a stupid fight.

❋

Chloe was in the middle of her cool-down stretches when she heard someone call out her name.

She turned. Kate stood there with Emily and Devin.

"Hey, Chloe," Kate said with a smile. "Are you busy? I wanted to talk to everyone for a second."

"Sure!" Chloe reached for her towel and glanced at Emily. Emily was watching her, too. Their eyes locked for a brief second before the girls turned away.

They sat down on the bleachers with Kate and Devin.

"So this is kind of related to cheerleading but kind of not," Kate began. "You know how I've been tutoring Adam's friend Willow? Well, her little sister, Sabrina, is having a birthday party this Sunday. She's going to be eight, and she really wants to be a cheerleader when she grows up. Willow asked if I could come to the party and teach Sabrina and her friends some cheers and stuff. Will you guys come with me?"

Chloe, Emily, and Devin all stared at Kate.

Emily was the first to speak. "Are you kidding? Why are you doing a favor for your number one enemy?"

"It's bad enough you have to tutor her," Chloe agreed.

"She's not my enemy anymore. She's been trying to get

along—sort of. And she doesn't flirt with Adam like she used to," Kate explained. "Besides, this isn't for her. It's for a bunch of future cheerleaders."

Chloe considered this. "Actually, I've been helping out some future cheerleaders, too."

"Really? Who?" Devin asked.

Chloe told the girls about Jasmyn and Beatrice. "I've met with them twice so far. They're really sweet and super-dedicated."

"That's so awesome that you're coaching them!" Kate said. "Hey, maybe they could come to Sabrina's birthday party, too. They could help us demonstrate motions and just help out."

"Yeah!" Devin exclaimed. "We could show Sabrina and her friends the basics. You know, like Cheerleading 101."

"Remember those cheers we used to do in your backyard when we were in sixth grade?" Emily reminded Chloe.

Chloe laughed. "We tried to copy whatever Jake and Clem did. I think my parents took videos in case we ever want to relive the humiliation."

"What humiliation? We were adorable!" Emily said merrily.

Everyone laughed.

They proceeded to brainstorm ideas for Sabrina's birthday party. Chloe got so caught up in the fun of planning the event that she almost forgot she and Emily were feuding. Or maybe the feud was over? They *were* finally talking to each other again, even if it was only about clasps, claps, and lunges.

Practice was almost finished. Coach Steele strolled to the center of the gym and blew her whistle.

"Listen up, people!" she called out.

Chloe and her friends stopped talking and whipped around to face the coach.

"It's just about quitting time. You've all done an excellent job today," Coach Steele went on. "Before I let you go, I wanted to make a couple of announcements. First of all, I just got our dates for this summer's cheer camp. Everyone who makes the JV or Varsity squad for next year should plan to attend. I've posted a link on the Northside website with the details, so feel free to check it out. I'll be registering everyone in late April, after tryouts are over and we have our new squads in place."

Cheer camp! Chloe felt a shiver of excitement. Camp last summer had been a blast, especially with Kate and Emily there. She couldn't wait to go again...

... *assuming* that she made the squad. But of course she would make the squad. It was only a matter of JV versus Varsity, wasn't it?

"Second, we've just selected our panel of judges for tryouts," Coach Steele continued. "There will be three judges total, like last year. But they will not be the same judges as before. And no, I cannot tell you who they are. Their identities are kept confidential until the day of. We don't want any of you sending them head shots or demo videos or presents to try to butter them up. Not that any of you would do anything like that."

Emily sputtered and coughed. She quickly grabbed for her water bottle, her face white as a sheet.

"Are you okay?" Chloe asked, concerned.

Emily nodded a little too eagerly. "Yup! I'm fine! Never better!"

Chloe frowned. What was up with Emily? Was she just nervous about tryouts? Or was it something more?

CHAPTER 12

"Hey, cheer people! Thanks for stopping by!"

Willow opened the front door and waved everyone inside. She wore a big, colorful hat shaped like a birthday cake and several strands of light-up Mardi Gras beads.

"Hey, Willow. Are we early?" Kate asked.

"Nah, you're right on time."

Kate made introductions all around. She, Emily, Chloe, and Devin were dressed in matching blue shell tops with NORTHSIDE embroidered across their chests in cursive and A-line skirts trimmed with white and gold. Jasmyn and Beatrice wore cheer T-shirts and camp shorts that they'd borrowed from Chloe. All six girls had pulled their hair back in neat ponytails with ribbons. Emily and Devin carried canvas bags filled with pom-pons.

The six of them followed Willow through the Zelinski family's ultramodern home. Kate loved the pristine, all-white décor. If this had been her house, there would be strawberry jam handprints all over the furniture, courtesy of her younger siblings. Vintage movie posters covered the walls, and hundreds of books filled the floor-to-ceiling bookshelves.

In the kitchen, Willow introduced her parents, who were both architects. Kate recognized Molly the cat and their golden retriever, Oliver, from Willow's sonnet.

Willow eventually led everyone to the backyard, where the party was taking place. Her eight-year-old sister, Sabrina, bounced up and down on a trampoline along with a few other kids. More kids played on the swing set. Several picnic tables were laden with pitchers of lemonade and platters of fresh fruit, bagels, and cupcakes. A bouquet of brightly colored balloons bobbed in the breeze.

Adam reclined on a lawn chair, blowing bubbles and watching over the younger children. He scrambled to his feet when he saw Kate and the others.

"Hey, Lady Kate!" He rushed up to her and gave her a big, warm hug. "I'm so happy to see you. My parents might stop by later."

Kate hugged him back. Adam and his family lived next

door in a large Tudor-style brick house. "I'm happy to see you, too. This is my cheer crew. We're the entertainment!"

Emily, Devin, Chloe, Jasmyn, and Beatrice waved to Adam.

Adam punched his arm in the air. "Go, Northside!"

Jasmyn and Beatrice followed suit. "Go, Northside!" they shouted together. Chloe gave them an approving nod.

Sabrina and her friends stopped what they were doing and came running up to Kate and the others.

"Are you the cheerleaders?" Sabrina asked eagerly.

Kate grinned. "Yes, we are! Who's ready to learn some motions and jumps?"

All seven kids raised their hands. "Me! Me! Me!" they cried out in unison.

Kate glanced over her shoulder at Chloe and Devin. It was a habit; they were her captains, and she was used to following their lead, not the other way around.

Chloe understood immediately. "Go ahead, Kate. You're the boss," she said with a smile. Devin nodded in agreement.

Kate smiled and nodded back. Then she turned to face the kids.

"All right, all right! Let's line up in a row. Birthday girl, you're in the center. We're going to begin with some basic motions and jumps. Then we'll put it all together and perform a cheer."

"Can we use those round, puffy things?" one of the boys asked.

Kate laughed. "You mean the poms? Yes, as soon as you learn the movements."

She decided to start with the beginning stance. This involved standing with your feet together, arms down at your sides, and fingertips straight down. Next was the cheer stance, which meant moving your feet to a little more than shoulder width apart; your upper body stayed the same as in the beginning stance. As Kate called out the motions, Chloe, Emily, Devin, Jasmyn, and Beatrice demonstrated.

After that came a bunch of simple arm motions: claps, clasps, overhead clasps, low clasps, high Vs, low Vs, touchdowns, low touchdowns, and tabletops. Once the kids got the basics, Kate led them in a game of Simon Says using the motions.

"Simon says, high V!" Kate called out, laughing as the kids quickly shot their arms into the air.

Once the game came to an end, Chloe, Emily, Devin, and Kate taught the group a simple cheer:

"LET'S..." (*Broken T*)
"GO" (*T motion*)
"TIMBER-" (*Drop arms*)
"WOLVES!" (*Right punch*)
(*Clap clap, clap clap clap*)

They repeated the cheer three times. Then Kate played the Northside fight song on her phone and taught the kids the words. They all sang happily together, clapping their hands and cheering.

At one point, Willow caught Kate's eye and mouthed, *Thank you.* Kate mouthed back, *You're welcome.* She was glad they were getting along better. At this rate, they might even become friends someday!

❋

"I think we were a huge hit," Chloe said to Emily, Devin, and Kate.

The four girls sat cross-legged on the grass, eating cupcakes and drinking lemonade. Across the yard, Sabrina opened her presents at the picnic table while her friends, parents, and big sister, Willow, watched. Adam had gone home with his parents, and Jasmyn and Beatrice had taken off, too.

"Remember when we were that age?" Kate remarked as Sabrina pulled a brand-new set of poms out of a gift bag and began jumping up and down with joy.

Emily grinned. "Oh, yeah. I wanted to be a cheerleader more than anything. As in, I would have traded a closetful of my favorite toys for a spot on the Northside squad someday."

Chloe nodded. "Me too. I remember when Clem gave me her old poms. I slept with them next to my pillow."

"How about you, Devin?" Kate asked curiously. "What were you like when you were eight?"

"I was different from you guys. I dreamed about becoming a top gymnast, not a cheerleader," Devin confessed. "In fact, I pretty much lived at my home gym. I saw more of my gymnastics coach than of my parents. Practices ran super-late. I did my homework during breaks, sitting on the sidelines. I ate dinner in the car on the drive home."

Emily whistled. "Wow, that's serious dedication."

"Do you miss it? Gymnastics, I mean?" Kate asked Devin.

"Actually, the thing is…" Devin paused and looked away.

Chloe, Kate, and Emily leaned in, waiting for Devin to go on.

"You know I've been practicing for tryouts at Synergy Gymnastics, right? On Mondays during their open gym time?" Devin said finally. "Well, a couple of their coaches, Mr. and Mrs. Logan, were kind of checking me out on the first day. They asked me to join their Level 8 team. They have a really important competition coming up."

"Wait, *what?*" Kate gasped. She couldn't believe Devin had managed to keep such big news to herself all this time!

"You said no, right?" Emily demanded.

Devin was silent. "Not exactly," she admitted. "I thought about it for a while. And I came really close to saying yes. I mean, this could be my chance to become a competitive gymnast." She added, "I'm still not a hundred percent sure about cheerleading versus gymnastics. But it doesn't matter. My sister convinced me that I can't join the Synergy team. The gym fees are super-expensive. There's no way my mom can afford them. Plus, Synergy is really far from my house, and I wouldn't have any way to get there for all the practices."

"What did the Logans say when you told them?" Kate asked.

"I haven't told them yet. I'm going to, though. Tomorrow," Devin replied.

"Whew! Call me selfish, but I'm so relieved you'll be staying on the squad," Emily said. "Northside needs you!"

Chloe frowned. "What do you care, Em? Devin's going for JV. You're going for Varsity. You know, as in different squads?" she pointed out testily.

Emily looked hurt. "You're going for Varsity, too!"

"Yeah, but I'd be fine with it if I didn't make Varsity. You, on the other hand, are totally obsessed with making the cut. You spend all your free time with Zoe Devereaux. You spy on the Varsity practices," Chloe accused.

"*Excuse* me?" Emily cried. "I don't spy! I attend and observe the practices. Zoe told me I should."

"Zoe, Zoe, Zoe," Chloe muttered under her breath.

"Um, guys? How about another cupcake?" Kate said

quickly. The four of them had been having so much fun up until now. She wanted to return to the happy mood of a minute ago.

"No, thank you." Chloe sniffed. "I have to go, anyway. It's getting late."

"I have to go, too," Emily said, rising to her feet. "Thanks for inviting me, Kate."

Emily and Chloe went over to say good-bye to Willow and Sabrina and their parents. Then Emily took off down the driveway. Chloe took off in a different direction.

Kate and Devin exchanged a glance. "What. Just. Happened?" Devin asked, her green eyes wide. "Everything was going so well!"

"I thought they'd made up, but I guess I was wrong," Kate replied with a sigh.

"Are they *ever* going to make up?"

"Honestly? I'm not sure anymore."

Across the yard, Sabrina and her friends got up from the picnic table and started performing a cheer for Oliver the dog and Molly the cat.

"T-E-A-M!" they shouted, punching the air. "Goooooo, team!"

Kate picked up another cupcake, broke it in half, and bit into it moodily. Their *own* team—their foursome—was falling apart by the minute. How were they going to save it?

CHAPTER 13

Devin hurried into Synergy Gymnastics on Monday after school. Sage was back at college, and Devin was already tired and cranky from the long commute. She'd had to change buses twice. The last one had taken forever to arrive, then dropped her off several blocks away.

"Hi!" Devin checked in at the front desk and gave five dollars to the receptionist, who was a different woman from the past two Mondays. Her hair fell in elaborate cornrows, and she wore a pretty rhinestone necklace that spelled DEVYN.

"Is that your name? Because I'm Devin, too. With an 'i,'" Devin said.

"It's nice to meet you, Devin with an 'i,'" Devyn replied with a wide grin. "But I already know who you are. You're famous around here!"

"Excuse me?"

"Mr. and Mrs. Logan have been talking about the amazing new girl from Northside who might join our gym. I really hope you do."

Devin glanced down at her sneakers, feeling awkward. Today was the day she was going to tell the Logans about her decision *not* to join their gym. "Thanks. That's nice of you to say."

"I mean it. We're like a family here. *And* we're the rockingest gym in SoCal. Check out those laurels." Devyn pointed to a nearby case that shimmered with dozens and dozens of gleaming trophies. "Plus, do you know about our famous alumni? We've had five—no, *six*—of our gymnasts go on to compete in the Olympics."

"Wow, that's incredible!"

"It sure is. Now go! Tumble your heart out! And don't forget to check out our new juice bar in the lounge area."

Devin thanked her and headed down the hallway.

She was beyond frustrated.

Six alumni in the Olympics. That really *was* incredible. The Logans obviously knew how to nurture young gymnasts and help them evolve into world-class competitors.

If only she'd met them last fall...

If only she lived nearby...

If only her mom was really, really rich...

Devin's old boyfriend, Josh, used to have a bumper sticker on his guitar case that read Bloom Where You're Planted. Josh had always been big on upbeat, motivational sayings. Devin was not, but this particular saying had stuck with her, and it felt relevant to her situation now.

She obviously needed to change her attitude and accept the fact that she was meant to bloom on the Northside JV squad—not at the very expensive and very faraway Synergy Gym.

Of course, Mateo would totally not agree with Josh's bumper sticker. He was more of a "go where the wind takes you" kind of guy.

"Devin! Hello!"

Devin glanced up to see Mrs. Logan standing in the doorway of the gym. Mrs. Logan beamed and waved, obviously happy to see her.

Devin waved back. "Hi, Mrs. Logan. I'm here for the open gym time."

"Wonderful! Do you have a few minutes to spare before you start throwing passes? I wanted to introduce you to some of the other kids on our Level 8 team. I know you still haven't made a decision about joining, but I thought it might be helpful to get their perspective," Mrs. Logan said.

"That's really nice of you. But, actually, um..." Devin hesitated.

"What is it, dear?"

"I've already made my decision. I can't. Join, I mean," Devin blurted out.

"Oh! I'm so sorry to hear that," Mrs. Logan said, sounding surprised. "I guess you're just a cheerleader at heart, huh?"

"No! I mean, not exactly."

"What is it, then?" Mrs. Logan asked curiously.

Devin tried to find the right words. "I really *like* being a cheerleader. More than I ever thought I would. But gymnastics is my first love," she began. "My parents got divorced last year. My sister, Sage, is in college. So it's just my mom and me in Sunny Valley. She works crazy hours as a nurse and she doesn't have the time to drive me all the way out here for practices. Plus, there's no way she can afford the club fees. We barely managed up in Spring Park where I'm from, and that was with my dad helping to pay for them, too. Now that they're divorced, things are...different." Devin didn't add that she often overheard her parents fighting on the phone about money, even now.

Mrs. Logan nodded slowly. "I think I understand. What you're saying is, if the fees and the commute weren't obstacles, you'd give up cheerleading for gymnastics?"

"I don't know. Maybe. I haven't had a chance to really think about one versus the other. All I know is that my family can't afford for me to go back to club gymnastics."

"Got it." Mrs. Logan glanced over her shoulder. "Why don't you go inside and warm up? I want to continue our conversation, but I have to check on something first. I'll be back in a sec."

"Sure."

Mrs. Logan squeezed Devin's arm, nodded to herself, and walked away. For a moment, Devin felt a pang of regret. She wished she could have said yes to Mrs. Logan. Or at least maybe. Saying no had been a lot harder than she thought it would be.

Sighing, Devin headed into the gym. She set her duffel bag down on a bench and began warming up. The gym was pretty full today, and she recognized some of the same faces from the last two Mondays. Leila was among them; she sat nearby, sipping from a water bottle and texting on her phone.

Leila glanced up and spotted Devin. Devin gave a little wave. Leila narrowed her eyes and returned to her texting.

What is that girl's problem? Devin wondered, not for the first time.

Devin was about to get up and start her practice session when she saw the Logans entering the gym and walking toward her.

"There she is!" Mr. Logan greeted her. "How are you doing, Devin? Did you get a chance to check out that article I mentioned about conditioning exercises for the vault?"

"I did! Thanks so much, Mr. Logan."

"No problem. I have another one I thought you'd like, about how to manage balance beam falls," he added.

"Thanks, Mr. Logan, but..." Devin glanced uncertainly at Mrs. Logan. "Didn't your wife tell you?"

"She did. And we have a plan we'd like to run by you," Mr. Logan replied.

"A plan?"

"Yes, and here it is. If you decide to join our team, we'd be happy to waive your club fees," Mr. Logan said. "We'll also arrange for a club family to drive you to and from practices. A couple of our Level 8 girls live near you."

"We're not pressuring you to join our team," Mrs. Logan added quickly. "We just want you to be able to say yes or no based on your own goals. We don't want details and logistics to get in the way."

Devin was stunned. "*Really?*" she managed after a moment.

"Really. Wendy's absolutely correct. We don't want someone as talented as you to have to throw away your dreams because of financial need or transportation challenges," Mr. Logan explained. "Anyway, nothing else has changed. Keep thinking. Discuss your options with your mom. Let us know if you have any questions. We don't need your final decision right this minute. Take till the second week of April. You can tell us then."

"No problem," Devin said. "Thanks so much, Mr. and Mrs. Logan!"

Mrs. Logan patted her arm. "Thank *you*, Devin."

Later, Devin sat in the lobby of the Synergy Gym, waiting for her ride. The Logans had invited her to stop by the Level 8 practice, where she'd met some of the team members, and watched them in action. They were good. *Really* good. Back at Rocket Gymnastics, Devin had probably been their number one gymnast, which had been cool, but had its limits. If she joined the Synergy team, she wouldn't be number one. She would be fifth or sixth, at best. Which meant that she would have room to grow and a high bar to reach for.

Bloom where you're planted. With their generous offer, the Logans had given her the option of blooming in two different places: either here with them or back at Northside with Coach Steele and the cheerleading squad.

Now, all she had to do was decide. By the second week of April. Which was the same time as cheerleading tryouts. *Yikes!*

Devin glanced at her watch. The Logans had arranged for her to drive home with the family of Lise Brownstein, who was on the Level 8 team and who lived just five minutes away from the Isles. Lise was a junior at Northside.

Her phone rang. MATEO flashed across the screen.

Devin hit Talk. "Hey!" she said happily.

"Hey. I wanted to see how you're doing. Did you talk to the Logans yet?"

"Yes! I told them I couldn't join their team because of the money and everything. But guess what?"

"What?"

"They offered me a scholarship! And they said they'd arrange for me to get rides to and from practice!"

Mateo laughed. "Wow. I can't say I'm surprised, though. You're, like, the most awesome gymnast ever. I'm sure the Logans would do anything to have you on their team."

"Aw, thanks. I don't think I'm the most awesome gymnast *ever*. But thanks."

"You're welcome. So what are you going to do?" Mateo asked her.

"I don't know," Devin admitted. "I have to think some more. And talk to my mom."

"Well, I'm here if you need me."

"Thanks."

"And no matter what you decide, we'll celebrate. Lobster Claw, crab cakes, my treat."

Devin's heart skipped. She was glad they were on the phone so that Mateo couldn't see her blushing.

Just then, another call came through. Coach Steele's name popped up.

Devin frowned. The coach never, ever called her. What could she possibly want?

"I have to go. Coach Steele is calling me," Devin told Mateo.

"Okay. I'll talk to you later."

"Definitely."

Devin hung up and picked up the second call. "Hello?"

"Devin? It's Meg Steele."

"Hi, Coach. How are you?"

"We need to talk," Coach Steele said in a serious-sounding voice. "Would it be convenient for me to stop by and speak to you and your mother? Say, around eight o'clock tonight?"

"Uh, sure," Devin replied. "Mom should be home from the hospital by then."

"Fine, I'll see the two of you at eight. Good-bye."

"Bye, Coach."

Am I in trouble? Devin wondered as she hung up.

CHAPTER 14

"Leila ratted me out," Devin told Emily the next day. "She eavesdropped on my conversation with the Logans yesterday. Then she called Coach Steele and told her I was going to quit cheerleading!"

The two girls sat in the cafeteria, eating lunch. Bright sunlight poured down through the skylights and made the blue-and-white walls gleam. Devin and Emily had been having lunch together all semester. Chloe and Kate had different schedules and ate later.

"That Leila Savett is seriously evil." Emily huffed. She broke a celery stick in half and nibbled on it furiously. "Wait. *Are* you going to quit cheerleading?"

"I don't know," Devin said, reaching into her bag of pita chips. "The Logans have basically offered me a scholarship, starting now, until I graduate from high school. That means free gymnastics for the next three years! Plus, they're arranging for me to get a ride to and from the practices. They want my decision by the second week of April."

"Because you don't have enough pressure already? That's the same time as tryouts," Emily pointed out.

Devin sighed. "Tell me about it. Anyway, Coach Steele came over to our house last night. She and my mom are old friends. To be fair, she was really nice about everything. She explained that I can't do both, which I already knew. She said she'll support my decision, either way." She added, "She's a pretty great coach. We're really lucky to have her on the JV squad."

Yeah, but for how long? Emily thought, remembering what Zoe had told her. She wished she could mention this juicy tidbit to Devin. But she'd promised Zoe. *Ugh.* Secrets were so hard to keep, especially such a big one.

"Life is so complicated," Emily said instead. "Like boys. They're complicated, too!" She giggled.

"I totally agree. About life, I mean. And boys, too," Devin said. "Although Mateo is pretty straightforward. He always says what he means, and he's not afraid to show his feelings, either."

"Thank you for reminding me that you have a perfect

boyfriend while some of us have no boyfriend whatsoever," Emily joked.

"He's not my—"

"Although, did I tell you about this superhot guy I met at Rockabella? He's come by the store two Saturdays in a row now. His name is Braden, and he's really nice. Did I mention that he's superhot? I did, didn't I? The only problem is, he goes to Breckenridge. *And* he's a senior. *And* he happens to be Nadine's son."

Devin made a face. "Nadine, your evil boss? Awkward."

"*Très* awkward. Did I mention that Braden speaks fluent French? He's been to Paris twice!"

"Sweet. Where's he going to college this fall?"

"He doesn't know yet. He said his first choice is USC. He wants to double major in economics and film. Did I mention that he used to be a child actor? And a model?"

"Sounds like someone's got a crush," Devin said in a singsong voice.

Emily blushed. "We're just friends, that's all. Although… if he asked me to go to the spring dance with him, I wouldn't say no. In fact, I already have my dress picked out. It's teal. Did I mention that teal is Braden's favorite color?"

"You did not. But teal would be really pretty on you. Even though it is a Breckenridge color."

"Oh, yeah. Oops."

Devin's phone buzzed. She slipped it onto her lap and

glanced at it surreptitiously. Texting wasn't allowed during school hours. The cafeteria monitor was standing several tables over, and he usually didn't miss a thing. Fortunately, he seemed to be distracted by a group of sophomores who were on the verge of a food fight.

"What's up? Is that your BF?" Emily asked Devin.

"He's not my—never mind. It's Chloe. She had a question about tonight's practice."

"Oh?"

Emily snapped another celery stick in half, and then in quarters. She wondered why Chloe wasn't texting *her* to ask about practice.

Oh, yeah. We're not speaking to each other.

Devin slipped her phone back into her pocket. "She wants to make sure that we spend some time going over our ground-up liberty. I totally agree. We really need to nail that stunt before tryouts."

"Uh-huh."

"Emily?" Devin leaned across the table and pointed to her tray. "Why are you destroying that poor celery stick? And why are you and Chloe still fighting? It can't be *that* bad, can it?"

Emily glanced down at the ragged chunks of celery on her tray. "I don't know. I'm not even sure why we're fighting. It's like she's mad because I'm trying out for Varsity, and because I'm spending so much time with Zoe."

"You *are* spending a lot of time with Zoe. But that's a good thing, right? It sounds like she's been helping you."

"Yeah, she's been great! Because of her, my cheering skills are one hundred percent improved. I can even throw a tuck now." Emily looked away. "The thing is . . . okay, I'm just going to spill. Zoe wants me to do something that I'm not totally comfortable with."

"What is it?" Devin asked curiously.

Emily took a deep breath. "There will be three judges at tryouts. You know that, right?"

"Uh-huh."

"And you know that their identities are top secret, right?"

"Uh-huh. So?"

"So Zoe found out the identity of one of the judges. She's Zoe's neighbor." Emily didn't want to mention Mrs. Van Dorn by name. "Apparently, she's looking for a babysitter for her twins. Zoe wants *me* to be their babysitter so that I can get the judge to like me."

Emily stopped and waited for Devin's reaction.

"Yeah, that's definitely not cool," Devin said after a moment. "I'm kind of surprised Zoe would suggest that. She should have faith in you. I mean, you'll make Varsity or JV based on *you*, not on who you know."

"Yes, exactly! I've been so confused, trying to figure out what to do. I mean, Zoe is supersmart about everything. I feel like I'm supposed to trust whatever she says. But this idea just doesn't *feel* right, you know?"

"I know!"

Emily smiled gratefully at Devin. It was so nice to be able to share her problems with a good friend. Especially since she and Chloe weren't talking these days.

At least Emily knew what she needed to do regarding the babysitting job. In fact, she was due over at Mrs. Van Dorn's house tonight after practice for an "interview." Emily would use that opportunity to say thanks, but no thanks.

❋

"Emily, we've been expecting you. Come in!"

Mrs. Van Dorn waved her into the house. She was tall and athletic looking, and she wore her long brown hair in a sleek ponytail. A ring of keys hung from a black lanyard around her neck.

As soon as Emily stepped through the door, she was hit in the face by a flying plastic triceratops. "*Ow!*" she cried out.

"Girls! That is a *big no*! What did we say about throwing toys inside the house?" Mrs. Van Dorn yelled.

Two small figures dashed across the hallway and vanished into another room. Emily could hear giggling and whispering.

"I apologize for my twins. Why don't you come into the kitchen? Zoe's already here."

"She is?" Zoe hadn't mentioned anything to Emily about that.

"Yes. She just got here."

Mrs. Van Dorn turned and led the way to the kitchen. Emily followed, barely noticing the carnage of toys and crayons scattered across the polished hardwood floors as she rehearsed her lines in her head:

I'd really love to babysit for you, but my parents need me to help out at home.

I have to spend more time on my schoolwork.

My cat's really sick.

Of course, Emily didn't have a cat. And her schoolwork was just fine. And her parents hadn't said a word to her about doing more chores around the house; she already did plenty, even more than Chris and Eddie, probably. Still, she wanted to sound smooth and graceful when she turned down the job.

Zoe was sitting at the kitchen counter flipping through a copy of *American Cheerleader* and picking at a bowl of mixed nuts. "Hey, Emily!"

"Hey, Zoe! What are you doing here?"

"I thought I'd stop by so I could tell Mrs. Van Dorn what an awesome babysitter you would be for Tia and Tessa," Zoe explained.

"Zoe spoke very highly of you," Mrs. Van Dorn piped up.

"Oh!"

Emily plastered a smile on her face. Zoe and Mrs. Van Dorn smiled back and waited for her to go on.

Emily felt frozen where she stood. What should she say? What should she do?

"Emily? Everything okay?" Zoe prompted her.

"Yes! I mean, no!"

Zoe frowned.

Emily turned to Mrs. Van Dorn. "I'd really love to baby-sit for you. Thank you so much for considering me. But my parents need me to help out more with their school-work…I mean, with our sick cat, Rover—I mean, *Grover*. And anyway, I can't. I'm sorry. But thank you! I'm really sorry!"

With that, Emily whirled around and made a beeline for the front door.

Whack! In the hallway, another plastic dinosaur hit her in the leg. Two blond heads peeked out from behind a large potted plant.

Emily rushed outside and closed the door behind her. So much for smooth and graceful. That definitely had not been her finest moment.

Still, she was relieved to be done with it. And now, she and Zoe could get back to their regular practices. At tryouts, Emily wanted the numbers on her score sheet to be about her skills, not her connections.

"*Emily!*"

Emily turned. Zoe had followed her outside.

She didn't look happy.

"Hey. What's up?" Emily asked, confused.

"*What's up?*" Zoe fumed. "I went out of my way to introduce you to an important person who could make or break your chances of moving up to Varsity. She was ready to hire you to babysit her two girls. But you just walked away from all that. And you have the nerve to ask me 'what's up'?"

Emily gasped. "But Zoe—"

"Forget it. I'm through. I'm done being your fairy godmother. From now on, Emily Arellano, you're on your own! Good luck at tryouts. At the rate you're going, you'll be on the JV squad for the rest of your life!"

CHAPTER 15

"Hey, Jasmyn! With a daggers motion, bring your fists in so that they're right in front of your shoulders. And Beatrice? Your hands should be right under your chin when you're doing a clasp motion," Chloe told the girls.

"Like this, Chloe?" Jasmyn tried the daggers motion again.

"Perfect!"

"How about me, Chloe?" Beatrice repeated her clasp.

"That's awesome! Now, let's go through our cheer again. And both of you, don't forget to keep your muscles tight and punch out with a lot of strength." Chloe clapped twice and raised her voice: "From the beginning!"

Jasmyn and Beatrice spread out on the Davises' perfectly

manicured lawn. On a four-count, they launched into the simple practice routine that Chloe had choreographed for them.

Chloe sat down on the steps of the back deck and watched the girls carefully. They were doing so well. Much better than when she had started working with them a few weeks ago. For one thing, Beatrice had come out of her shell and really started projecting her voice. And both girls had quickly grasped the importance of the fundamentals: clean motions, strong jumps, big smiles, and a lot of enthusiasm.

Now, all Chloe had to do was make sure they could nail the requirements: a back handspring for their standing tumbling and a round-off back handspring for their running tumbling. She also planned to spend a couple of afternoons coaching them with their stunt group, which included two other girls from Jefferson Middle School.

They went through the routine once, twice, three times. In between, Chloe gave them general technique pointers. She reminded them to keep their shoulders relaxed, their wrists straight, and their thumbs in the correct position during motions. She also reviewed the appropriate arm placement for their high Vs so that they didn't sink into Ts.

After a while, Jasmyn and Beatrice took a break. "What's it like to be a JV cheerleader?" Jasmyn asked as she toweled off her face.

"It's awesome. Because it's JV, we're all still learning. And we're all really supportive of each other," Chloe replied.

Except for Leila, she corrected herself mentally. But Leila Savett was definitely the exception to the rule and not worth mentioning.

Chloe smiled brightly and continued.

"I've seen the other girls on the squad really grow and change this year. Like my friend Kate, who you met last Sunday? At Sabrina's birthday party? She's a lot more confident than she was last fall. Cheerleading can make people feel good about themselves."

"Really?" Beatrice perked up.

"Really! Also, our squad does a huge amount of community service. I love that," Chloe went on. "Each season, we pick a charity to support. We have car washes, bake sales, raffles, stuff like that. And back in January, we organized a fashion show at the high school to raise money for a local family who were about to lose their home." She added, "Some of us also do extra volunteer work on the side. For example, Kate and I volunteer most Saturdays at this place called Hearts Heal—we were there earlier today. Kate does peer tutoring at school, too."

"What about Coach Steele? What's she like?" Beatrice asked.

"Coach Steele is fantastic. We wouldn't have made it to Nationals without her. She's tough, but she cares about us. She thinks of the squad as her family." Chloe paused. "We *are* a family."

"Wow." Jasmyn sighed dreamily. "Being a JV cheer-leader sounds like the most amazing thing in the world."

"Yeah, it kind of is," Chloe replied.

So why was she trying out for Varsity?

Later that afternoon, Chloe lay on her bed, listening to a mix on her iPod and finishing up her history homework. Bruno Mars didn't exactly go with the Battles of Saratoga and the rest of the Revolutionary War, but it made the time pass more easily. Valentine slept at her feet, thumping her tail contentedly.

It had been a long day. Chloe had spent two hours volunteering at Hearts Heal in the morning, and she'd devoted most of her afternoon to coaching Jasmyn and Beatrice.

And now, homework. She would have to think of something fun to do to unwind later—maybe a movie marathon on TV or a dip in the heated infinity pool. She could call Kate and invite her over. Although Kate usually spent her Saturday nights with Adam.

The front doorbell rang. Valentine woke up and began barking. Mr. Davis called up: *"Chloe!* Your friend's here!"

Friend? Had Jasmyn or Beatrice forgotten something?

Chloe snapped her history textbook shut and sat up on her bed. She heard footsteps coming up the stairs.

A second later, Emily poked her head through the door. "Hey. Hi. Are you busy?" she asked hesitantly.

Chloe bit back her surprise. *What is Emily doing here?*

They hadn't spoken to each other since the party last Sunday—except at practice, and even then, their conversations had been perfunctory, just details about the ground-up liberty that the two of them were working on with Kate and Devin. They'd exchanged a few texts and e-mails about the music for the spring dance, but that was it.

Chloe lowered her eyes and stared at her history book. "I'm super-busy," she mumbled, opening it up to some random chapter and pretending to read. "Test on Monday."

"Sorry. I just got off my shift at Rockabella, and I thought I'd stop by."

"Oh. How's your new BFF Zoe?"

"She's not my best friend. She's not even my friend. Not anymore."

Chloe raised her eyebrows. "What happened?"

"It's a long story. Anyway, I'm here about the spring dance. You've been looking at all the band demos yourself. I'm sorry. I kind of dropped the ball."

"Yeah, kind of."

"Hey, Chloe? Your book's upside down."

"What?"

"Your history book. It's upside down. It might be easier to read if you turned it right-side up."

"Oh!" Blushing, Chloe flipped the book around. "Yeah, that's better. So, um...what were you saying?"

"I was going to say, if you have a list of the band demos you still have to look at, I could take over," Emily offered.

Chloe considered this. She took a deep breath. Then another.

Emily was making an effort. Maybe she should make an effort, too.

"Yeah, I have a list. Are you free now? We could finish the job together," Chloe said finally.

Emily's face lit up. "Really?"

"Really. I was just about to make some popcorn. Are you hungry?"

"I'm starving!"

Before long, Chloe and Emily were sitting in the Davises' living room, munching on popcorn and laughing hysterically at a YouTube video of a local band called Animal Farm.

"Do they actually think those dorky cow hats are cool?" Chloe remarked.

"And what about that weird move the lead guitarist makes every time he plays a solo? He looks like he's about to throw up." Emily guffawed.

"I don't think Animal Farm is going to make the cut, do you?"

"Definitely not. *Next!*"

Chloe clicked to another video. This one was by a girl band called the Cupcake Zombies. *Hmm, not bad.* Their sound was a perfect blend of pop and edgy.

"I like them!" she and Emily said at the same time.

They glanced at each other and grinned.

"My brother knows their drummer. Maybe he can convince them to give us a discount?" Emily mused.

"Which brother? You mean Chris? How is he, anyway?" Chloe asked.

Emily giggled. "Actually, it's Eddie. But Chris is fine. Do you want his phone number so you can send him a flirty text?"

Chloe giggled, too. "*Stop* it!"

"Chris went to a movie tonight with some girl named Quinn. I'm not sure what their relationship status is. I could find out for you, though," Emily offered.

"Quinn Cummings? I thought she was dating that guy on the football team. Fernando something."

"Oooh, complicated! Is Quinn cheating on Fernando with Chris? Or is Quinn interested in Chris but he just likes her as a friend? Let me look into this."

As Emily typed away on her phone, Chloe grabbed another handful of popcorn and leaned back on the couch. She felt more relaxed than she had in a long time. Maybe she and Emily hadn't worked out all their issues. And who knew what would happen at tryouts in a week and a half. That would definitely be an opportunity for new drama.

But for now, they were hanging out and joking and laughing. That was progress.

And someday, they might even go back to being BFFs.

CHAPTER 16

"I can't go to the silent film festival with you this afternoon," Kate told Adam over the phone. "I'm really sorry. I know how much you were looking forward to it."

"Wait, why? They're showing *City Lights*, which is one of my favorites," Adam replied. "*And* it's at the Cinemania Theater, which you've never been to. You have to check out the red velvet seats! And instead of a sound track, this Austrian guy named Gustav plays live music on an ancient organ!"

"Yeah. I wish I could." Kate sat down on the living room floor, stretched out her legs, and leaned forward to touch her toes. She watched out of the corner of her eye as her little sister, Sasha, tried to dress their dog, Scout, in her ballet clothes. Sasha had stuck a frilly pink tutu on top of his head and draped several pair of tights around his neck.

"It's just that I'm having a minor panic attack," Kate went on. "Clinics start in eight days, and tryouts are in ten. I'm nowhere close to being ready. I need to spend today practicing."

"Why? You're perfect."

"I'm not. I'm far from it, in fact. My round-off back handspring is still shaky, and I need to work on my jumps, too."

There was a long silence on the other end of the phone.

"Adam? Are you there?"

"Yeah. Hang on, Lady Kate. I'm thinking."

Kate shifted her phone from one ear to the other. Her brothers, Garrett and Jack, ran by, slicing the air with foam pirate swords. Her parents sat at the dining room table drinking coffee, reading the Sunday paper, and listening to jazz on the radio.

She wished she'd devoted more hours to preparing for tryouts, like Chloe, Devin, and Emily. Even though Zoe wasn't helping Emily anymore—Emily had mentioned some big falling-out between the two of them—she was still in better shape than Kate.

Sure, Kate had attended the Tuesday and Thursday practices. But that was pretty much it. The rest of her free time had been taken up by her schoolwork, various volunteer jobs, and Adam. She had to get her head back in the game now that tryouts were right around the corner.

Or maybe she should bail altogether and skip cheerleading for sophomore year? Coach Steele had been crystal clear: just because someone was on the JV squad now didn't guarantee that she could *stay* on the squad. Kate knew she'd be competing against a whole new slew of candidates on April ninth. She didn't want to embarrass herself—

"Kate?" Adam's voice interrupted her thoughts.

"I'm here."

"Okay, so here's the deal. You need to come over to my house. Like, right now."

"What? No! I just told you, I can't hang out with you this afternoon. I really, really need to practice."

"It's okay. I have a plan. Meet me in my backyard."

"But—"

"Just trust me," Adam pleaded.

Kate sighed. How was she supposed to say no to that?

"I'll only stay for a moment," Kate murmured under her breath as she walked down the Findlays' driveway. Gardenia bushes lined the sides of their elegant Tudor-style house and filled the air with their sweet, heavy scent. She zipped up her hoodie, even though it was a balmy afternoon. She wanted to keep her muscles warm. From somewhere in the neighborhood, she could hear kids splashing in a pool.

When Kate reached the backyard, she stopped—and stared. Adam wasn't alone. Willow was there, too, along with a twenty-something woman Kate didn't recognize.

"You must be Kate!" the woman said in a friendly voice. She had short, spiky black hair and wore neon-pink sneakers.

Adam wrapped his arm around Kate's shoulders. "Yes. This is *the* Kate. The one I'm always waxing poetic about."

Willow rolled her eyes. "You are such a cornball, Finland."

"And you are such a buzz kill, Wills," Adam shot back.

"I'm Melissa. Adam's sister," the woman said, stepping forward and extending her hand.

"Hey, Melissa!" Kate shook her hand. She had actually never met any of Adam's siblings before. She remembered that Melissa lived and worked in Sunny Valley somewhere, and that another sister, Alice, was away at college in Seattle.

Adam smiled at Kate. "You're probably wondering why I asked you to come over."

"Yeah. I'm a little confused," Kate admitted.

"Melissa's a youth gymnastics coach. She's here to help you nail your round-off backward whatever and all the other complicated, twisty-turny stuff you have to do for tryouts," Adam explained.

Kate stared at Melissa. "No way. Really?"

Melissa nodded. "Really. I'm going to work your butt off this afternoon. By the time we're through, you'll be more than ready for those judges."

"Wills and I will cheer you on from the sidelines. Get it? We're going to be *your* cheerleaders!" Adam joked.

"Aw." Kate hugged Adam, then turned to Melissa and Willow. "This is so nice of you guys. Thank you!"

"You haven't even heard the best part yet. I wrote you a poem. You know, to inspire you at your trial," Willow piped up.

"*Tryout*. Really, you wrote me a poem?"

"Yeah. I'm still not sure why you want to be a cheerleader. It's, like, the lamest thing ever. But I thought you could use some extra inspiration. So here goes."

Willow pulled a crumpled piece of paper out of her pocket. She cleared her throat and began reading out loud:

POEM
By Willow Zelinski

There once was a cheerleader named Kate,
Who had a hard time believing she was great,
But when the big day arrived
She not only survived
But she outdid herself and changed the course of her fate.

Kate beamed. "Omigosh, you wrote that? For me?"

"Yeah. You're not going to correct my iambic pentameter or whatever, are you?" Willow asked her suspiciously.

"No, it's wonderful. Thank you so much." Kate gave Willow a hug, too. She was glad that the two of them had managed to become friends, after everything.

"Oh, whatever. I figured I should do something for you, since you helped me get a B plus on my sonnet." Willow patted Kate on the back.

"Okay, enough with the love. It's time to get to work. Kate, why don't you warm up, and then let's see where you're at with your tumbling," Melissa said.

"Yes, Coach!"

Kate unzipped her hoodie and began doing some hamstring stretches on the grass.

Maybe she wouldn't have to bail on tryouts, after all.

CHAPTER 17

"How long have you been with the Logans?" Devin asked Lise Brownstein curiously. It was Monday night, and they sat at the Synergy juice bar together, drinking mango smoothies. Devin had spent an hour practicing for cheerleading tryouts during the open gym time, then spent the next hour tumbling with the Level 8 gymnastics team. Lise's dad had given the girls a ride to Synergy and would be picking them up as well.

"Since I was in diapers. Just kidding, but sometimes it feels like that," Lise replied with a twinkle in her hazel eyes. "My parents signed me up for the Li'l Tots Tumbling classes when I was in preschool. I was good at it, and I really loved it, too. It was a way for me to work out all that crazy little-kid energy. When I was in second grade, I got my first trophy. I thought it was the best day of my life!" She added, "Now, gymnastics *is* my life. I can't imagine not doing it. It's my number one priority. And if I'm lucky, I'll be able to continue through college and after college."

"So you want to be a competitive gymnast?"

"Oh, yeah. Big-time. The Logans said I have a shot at a scholarship, too. The college application season starts this fall and they have contacts at some of the top NCAA schools. They also know this awesome videographer who's going to make my demo video."

"Wow." Devin took a sip of her smoothie as she mulled this over. Talking to Lise really confirmed what she'd already suspected. The Logans were amazing coaches. And Synergy was an amazing club. If Devin decided to choose gymnastics, this would definitely be the place for her, especially since the Logans had offered her such a generous package.

The problem was deciding. With a week to go until cheerleading clinics and tryouts, Devin was still on the fence. On the one hand, the Logans were handing her a possible future in gymnastics on a silver platter. On the other hand, Devin really liked being a cheerleader. She'd even enjoyed being cocaptain with Chloe this past year. Amazingly, she and Chloe had learned to lead side by side with their different but complementary styles.

Devin smiled. A year ago, she would never have thought of herself as a leader. The only leading she'd ever done was ordering her cat, Emerald, around.

"Hello, girls!"

Devin turned. Mrs. Logan walked up to the juice bar.

"Devin, I saw you trying out the balance beam earlier. You seemed so comfortable. It's like you never left!"

"Thanks! I'd forgotten how different it is to do a back handspring on the beam versus on the floor."

"Well, you looked flawless from where I was standing. Sweetheart, do you have a minute?"

Lise grinned and jumped off the stool. "I know when I'm not wanted. Besides, I think I hear the vault calling my name. See you later!"

"Good luck!" Devin turned to Mrs. Logan. "Lise is super-nice. So are her parents. Thank you again for introducing me to them."

"Of course! The Brownsteins said they'll be happy to drive you to and from here as often as you need." Mrs. Logan sat down next to Devin. "I was wondering whether you've made your decision yet. I know that cheerleading tryouts are next week, so you must have a lot on your mind."

"Yeah." Devin hesitated. "I still haven't decided. I'm sorry. I know that you and Mr. Logan are waiting for my answer. I just have a lot to think about."

"I know you do, dear. And if there are any questions we can answer for you, don't hesitate to ask. You have such a bright future in gymnastics. We just want to help you make it happen."

"Thanks, Mrs. Logan."

"We absolutely don't want to pressure you. But we do have to send our final team list to the tournament folks by next Wednesday. The deadline is six PM. So we'll need to have your final decision by then."

Next Wednesday. That was the day of tryouts. By six PM, she wouldn't even know if she'd made next year's JV squad.

"No problem, Mrs. Logan. I'll have my answer to you by then," Devin promised.

Mrs. Logan stood up and patted her on the shoulder. "I know you'll make the right choice. You're going to be a star, Devin. Joe and I feel lucky to know you, whatever you decide."

Devin smiled uncertainly. She didn't feel like a star. She just felt confused.

❄

"Okay, let's run our stunt again," Devin called out.

Chloe, Emily, and Kate nodded as they assumed their positions on the mat. Chloe and Kate were bases, with Chloe being the main base and Kate the side base. Devin was the back spot, and Emily was the top.

It was Tuesday after school—and only eight days to try-outs. The other JV cheerleaders were spread out on the floor, practicing their own stunts, jumps, motions, and tumbling.

The ground-up liberty was difficult. *Really* difficult. It also involved a huge amount of unconditional trust. Devin and her friends had not been able to get it right since they started working on it together a few weeks ago.

The four girls assumed the ground-up position, which was like the one for an extension prep but with different grips. Devin put her right hand on Emily's right ankle, and her left hand under Emily's seat. Chloe held Emily's right foot in a prep grip. Kate supported Emily's right foot as well, with one hand, while she clasped Chloe's wrist with the other.

Then came the tricky part—actually, one of *several* tricky parts. On a one-two count, Devin quickly pushed Emily upward. Emily rose to a standing position with her hips over her knees, bent over slightly and holding on to Chloe and Kate's shoulders. *Success!*

It was time for the big finale. Devin called out: "One, two, down, up!" On the word *down*, all four girls dipped down slightly. On the word *up*, Emily rose swiftly to a standing position, locked out her right leg, and placed her left foot on the opposite knee. She flung her arms up in a high V. Chloe, Kate, and Devin extended through their arms and legs and looked up at Emily.

One second...two seconds...three seconds...

Emily held her position. Devin had to resist the impulse to pump her fist and shout: *"Yes!"* The four girls stood as still as statues and smiled out at their invisible audience.

It was finally time for the dismount. Back on the ground, Emily shouted, "Guys, we *did* it! *Finally!*"

Chloe draped her arm around Emily's shoulders. "You were amazing! Except for when you almost took out my face with your knee. Oh, and your socks smell."

"Liar! My technique was perfect. And my socks don't smell."

"Okay, your technique was perfect. But your socks *do* smell."

They cracked up as they went off in search of Gatorade. Devin and Kate exchanged a surprised glance. When had the two girls made up?

"Wow. Mom and Dad aren't fighting anymore," Devin remarked to Kate.

"I know! It feels like we're a team again—you know, our little team of four," Kate said, brushing back a lock of hair.

"Yeah." Devin smiled wistfully as she watched Chloe and Emily pulling drinks out of a cooler. She wondered: Could she leave all this behind? She'd built friendships. And bonds. And a sense of place among all the other cheerleaders. This was her world now.

But gymnastics used to be her world, and it could be again.

What was she going to do?

CHAPTER 18

The first day of clinics had finally arrived.

Emily glanced around the Northside gym nervously. Everything was changing so fast. Just last week, this had been *their* gym—hers and Chloe's and the rest of their squad's. Today, it was filled with new faces: not just the JV and Varsity girls but also some random Northside students and several dozen eighth graders. And in approximately forty-eight hours, two brand-new, handpicked squads would emerge.

Who would make the cut for JV? For Varsity? And where would she land?

Emily took a deep breath and shook out her arms,

willing her anxiety to go away. Chloe, Kate, and Devin all smiled encouragingly at her.

I'm glad the four of us are doing this together, Emily thought.

The assistant coach from Breckenridge, Mr. Piretti, strolled through the gym doors. Emily wondered what was happening with the Varsity coach job. Would it go to Coach Steele, Mr. Piretti, or someone else altogether?

Coach Steele stepped up to the front of the crowd. The two senior Varsity girls, Zoe and Mallory, flanked her. Zoe's gaze slanted in Emily's direction. Their eyes locked briefly before Zoe turned away, her expression ice-cold. Emily winced. She'd pretty much gotten over her friendship fail with Zoe, but not entirely.

Coach Steele raised her megaphone in the air and spoke into it: "Welcome, everyone! It's great to see so many faces here. For those of you who don't know me, I'm Meg Steele. I'm the Varsity and JV cheerleading coach here at Northside High."

The entire room erupted in a cacophony of claps and cheers. Several people shouted: "Go, Timberwolves!"

"I appreciate your collective enthusiasm," Coach Steele said with a broad grin. "Make sure to bring it to the floor over the next few days. Because you will have your work cut out for you, ladies and gentlemen. As you know, we will be running our clinics today and tomorrow, from after school until approximately six PM. Zoe Devereaux and Mallory Stein here are my graduating seniors. For the past few weeks, they have been helping me to choreograph your tryout cheer and dance. Today, we will be breaking you up into two groups, so they can teach them to you."

"I hope we don't get Zoe," Chloe whispered to Emily.

"I know," Emily whispered back. She had filled Chloe and Kate in on her entire Zoe saga over the weekend—and updated Devin, too. She hadn't mentioned Mrs. Van Dorn by name, though. She also hadn't told them that Coach Steele might not be the JV coach next year.

"Tomorrow, Zoe and Mallory will review the cheer and dance with you," Coach Steele went on. "You can also run through your tumbling passes, practice your jumps, and work with your stunt groups. By the way, if anyone does *not* have a stunt group to try out with yet, please come and see me. I will arrange for you to be in a group. I should also mention—if you want to stunt with more than one group, so that you can showcase different talents, you're welcome to do that. For example, feel free to stunt with one group as a main base and another group as a back spot. But you can only designate one stunt as your actual tryout stunt. I hope that's clear."

Everyone nodded.

"Any questions?" Coach Steele asked.

A boy in the front row raised his hand. "I have one!"

Emily recognized him from around Northside; she thought he might be a sophomore. "What's going to be happening on Wednesday, exactly?"

"Thank you for asking. On Wednesday, please check in no later than three o'clock at the registration table. At that time, you will receive your numbers, which you will attach to your shirts. After a warm-up period, the tryouts will begin. They will be divided into five parts. First, the new cheer, which I just mentioned. Then the new dance. Then tumbling. Then jumps. Then, finally, the stunts. You will perform when your number is called. And most important"—Coach Steele punched the air for effect—"you will knock the judges' socks off!"

There were more claps and cheers.

Coach Steele pulled an index card out of her pocket and scanned it quickly. "All right then. Let me briefly explain the scoring system that the judges will be using," she went on. "Your cheer will count for a maximum of twenty points. This includes up to five points for motions, five for facial expressions and enthusiasm, five for how well you project your voice, and five for your incorporated skills. Your dance is ten points, maximum. Jumps count for a possible total of ten points, which means up to three points for a toe touch, three for a hurdler, two for a Herkie, and two for a pike. Tumbling is a maximum of twenty total points, which means up to ten points for your standing tumbling and ten for your running tumbling. By the way, a layout can get you up to five extra points, and a full, ten extra points. And finally, with your stunts, the maximum is ten points for a full up, five for a liberty, and three for an extension. Finally, you can get up to ten points for overall impression and fifteen for teacher recommendations and GPA."

She added, "I know, I know. It's a lot of numbers. But please don't worry about the math. That's the judges' job, and they'll be bringing their calculators. You just concentrate on performing to the best of your abilities."

"I forgot that the running tumbling counted for ten points," Kate whispered, looking worried.

"Don't sweat it. You're going to nail this," Devin whispered back.

"Definitely," Emily said. Chloe squeezed Kate's arm.

"Are there any more questions?" Coach Steele peered around. "No? Then let's get this party started! Everyone to the left of this line"—she pointed to the half-court delineation—"will be in Zoe's group. Everyone to the right will be in Mallory's."

Oh no! Emily was in Zoe's group—and so were her friends.

"Maybe we should pretend we were standing on Mallory's side the whole time," Chloe suggested.

"Nah. Coach Steele will know. I swear, the woman has eyes in the back of her head. Let's just make the best of it," Emily replied.

* * *

Chloe caught her breath after completing her last right punch. "Yell D," she murmured to herself, practicing the words to the tryout cheer Zoe had just taught their group.

"Whew, this is a lot of work," Kate said, taking a swig of her sports drink. "I can't figure out those double pirouettes in the dance! I'm going to have to practice them at home tonight."

"Double pirouettes? Yikes! I thought they were singles," Emily gasped.

Devin mopped her forehead with a towel. "I messed up on my counting between motions. That Katy Perry song tripped me up."

"It's got a tricky beat in that one part," Chloe agreed.

Zoe clapped her hands. "Listen up, gang! Let's run through the tryout cheer again!" she called out.

Everyone took their places. On a count of four, they launched into the cheer, which was a defense sideline cheer:

"YELL D!"

They all stood with their feet apart and hit a right half low V.

"YELL D!"

They switched to the other side.

"YELL D!"

The group hit a high V.

"YELL D-E-!"

They bent their right arms straight back.

"YELL -FENSE!"

They finished with a right punch.

Zoe nodded slowly. "Hmm. Good but not perfect. Your motions need to be crisper. And don't forget the purpose of a defense sideline cheer. Imagine that the Northside football team is ahead 12–7 with just seconds on the clock. The other team is only ten yards away from a touchdown. If they succeed, the score will be 12–13 and we could lose. We have to stop them! *Defense!*"

"*Defense!*" everyone shouted back.

They ran the cheer several more times before switching to the tryout dance. On the other side of the gym, Mallory's group was doing the same. As Emily hopped and twirled to Katy Perry's new single, she wondered if she had what it took to make Varsity. If the answer was no, would she be really disappointed?

On the other hand, what if she made Varsity and Chloe didn't? What would that do to their friendship?

"Focus, Arellano!" Zoe said, cupping her hands over her mouth.

Emily snapped to attention. Zoe gave her a stern look before turning away to observe a line of eighth graders.

In part, Emily wanted to make Varsity just to spite Zoe. She knew that wasn't the most mature attitude in the world, but still. She would take whatever motivation she could get. Tryout day was going to be the toughest challenge of her life.

CHAPTER 19

It was tryout day. Or, as Chloe had typed into her calendar: THE DAY.

She had asked Jasmyn and Beatrice to meet her in the Northside girls' locker room so she could help them get ready. The two had worn gold shorts, white socks, and cheer shoes. Coach Steele had a rule against wearing Northside or cheer camp attire for tryouts, since she didn't want the judges to know who had cheerleading experience and who didn't. "I want everyone to be a blank slate on tryout day," she had explained to the group during clinics.

"Does my hair look okay?" Jasmyn asked Chloe. "I wasn't sure if I should wear a ribbon or what."

Chloe inspected Jasmyn's bow. It seemed a little limp and sad. She retied it quickly to make it more perky. "Perfect! And now, let's wipe off some of that sparkly gold eye shadow. It *is* one of the Northside colors, which is awesome. And it may be the right look for a school dance. But we need to be a little more understated for tryouts. Basically, it should be the same as our game-day makeup."

"Omigosh! I didn't know!" Jasmyn grabbed a tissue and swiped at her eyelids.

Beatrice crossed her arms over her chest. Her face was as pale as a sheet, and beads of sweat dotted her forehead. "I...feel...sick," she moaned.

"Are you *really* sick? Or are you super-nervous-feel-like-throwing-up sick?" Chloe asked, concerned.

"Um...the second one," Beatrice replied, holding up two fingers.

Chloe gave Beatrice a quick hug. "I know how you feel. I've been there. Just keep telling yourself, 'I'm going to be okay.'"

"I'm going to be okay, I'm going to be okay, I'm going to be okay," Beatrice recited in a queasy voice.

Chloe turned to Jasmyn and gave her a quick hug, too. Then she stepped back and regarded both girls. "You guys have been working really, really hard. You're ready. I know you're ready. So just take some deep breaths, smile as big as the sun, and believe in yourselves. Because *I* believe in you, one hundred and ten percent!"

"You're the best, Chloe!" Jasmyn exclaimed.

"The best!" Beatrice agreed.

Chloe flushed with pleasure. "Aw. Come on, guys. Group huddle!"

The three girls bent their heads together and wrapped their arms around one another's shoulders.

"We can do this!" Chloe chanted.

"*We can do this!*" Jasmyn and Beatrice repeated.

"Go, Timberwolves!"

"*Go, Timberwolves!*"

Afterward, Chloe made a few more tweaks: T-shirts tucked in, all accessories off, and a little Vaseline on the teeth to remind them to smile. As she followed Jasmyn and Beatrice out of the locker room, she felt like a mother hen. She was proud of them. But she was scared for them, too. Despite their attempts to be brave, they were obviously nervous. She remembered *her* first cheerleading tryouts, last spring. She, too, had been super-nervous-feel-like-throwing-up sick in this very locker room just before she'd had to hit the floor.

Even now, she didn't feel totally sure of herself—and this was with games, pep rallies, Regionals, Nationals, and cocaptain under her belt. She would be trying out with new skills that she'd just mastered in the past month or so. And she was up against some truly fierce competition...

I'm going to be okay, she told herself, clenching her fists at her sides. *I'm going to be okay, I'm going to be okay.*

⁕

Inside the gym, Chloe, Jasmyn, and Beatrice made their way through a crowd of prospective cheerleaders and headed over to the registration table. Several parent volunteers signed them in and gave them their numbers, which were being assigned randomly.

"I'm number one? Seriously?" Chloe gasped when the volunteer, whose name tag read MRS. THOMPSON, handed her number to her. Coach Steele didn't let the parents of the cheerleaders work the tryouts, since they tended to be too emotionally invested in the proceedings.

"I'm sure being number one is a good omen," Mrs. Thompson told Chloe brightly.

Chloe wasn't so sure about that. If the process was anything like it had been last year, Coach Steele would divide everyone up into groups of four for the cheer, dance, and jumps portions: one through four, five through eight, nine through twelve, and so on. The standing and running tumbling portions would be done individually, which meant that Chloe would be the very first person to go. *Yikes!* The order of the stunt groups was a little more complicated, especially since some people might stunt with more than one group. But in any case, Chloe's group, including Kate, Emily, and Devin, would be up first because of Chloe's number.

"Peel off the back and attach it to the front of your shirt," Mrs. Thompson instructed her.

"Okay." Chloe's hands shook slightly as she applied the number.

"The other way," Mrs. Thompson said.

Chloe glanced at it. It was upside down. She ripped it off, smoothed it out, and reapplied it. "Thanks, Mrs. Thompson."

"Of course. Good luck, honey."

Chloe lingered at the registration table, waiting for Jasmyn and Beatrice to get their numbers. Jasmyn drew seventeen. Beatrice's was twenty-one. Chloe did the math in her head. Jasmyn and Beatrice would likely get to try out together during the cheer, dance, and jumps portions. That was a plus and would give them some extra confidence. She was happy for them.

Still... number one?

Chloe led Jasmyn and Beatrice over to the corner of the gym, where Emily, Devin, and Kate were warming up. The three girls already had their numbers on their shirts. Emily was five, Devin was twenty-two, and Kate was fifty-two.

"I'll have to wait forever for my turn," Kate said anxiously, touching the front of her shirt.

"Yeah, but it'll give you more time to breathe and to visualize," Devin pointed out. Coach Steele had taught them the importance of mentally picturing a perfect cheer, stunt, pass, or whatever *before* actually doing it.

"How're you two feeling?" Emily asked Jasmyn and Beatrice.

"Terrified," Jasmyn blurted out.

"Me too," Beatrice added.

"Don't be. You guys are gonna rock!" Emily told them.

"Definitely," Chloe agreed.

As the six of them warmed up, Chloe surveyed the gym. Everyone on the JV squad was present, including Leila, who walked through her tryout cheer while moving her lips, looking more nervous than usual. Chloe waved to her with what she hoped was an encouraging smile. In spite of everything that had gone down between them, Chloe was still the JV cocaptain, and it was up to her to make sure her fellow cheerleaders were okay. Leila ignored her and continued with her silent, solitary cheer.

Oh, well, Chloe thought. At least she'd tried.

On the other side of the gym, the three judges sat at a long table in an area that had been cordoned off with ropes. Chloe recalled Emily's story about one of the judges and the babysitting job. Chloe was really glad that Emily had come to her senses and not followed Zoe's advice.

A short while later, after everyone had completed the

registration process, Coach Steele walked out onto the floor and blew a whistle. "First things first. Is there anyone here who isn't trying out? Besides our judges and volunteers, that is. If so, I'm afraid I have to ask you to leave the gym. These tryouts are not open to the public."

A handful of students stood up from the bleachers. Kate's boyfriend, Adam, and Devin's friend Mateo were among them.

As he walked out, Adam held up a large handmade sign that read GOOD LUCK, LADY KATE! in old-fashioned script. Kate blushed and gave him a little wave.

Coach Steele turned to face the rest of the crowd. "Okay, then. Now that we've got that squared away, I want to welcome you to the tryouts for the Northside JV and Varsity squads. I know you're all eager to get started. But before we do, I want to say a few words. First of all, I want you to enjoy yourselves today. I know that may sound impossible because there's so much at stake. But your hours and hours of practice and preparation are behind you now. When your number is called, just relax, smile, and do your thing. Have fun!"

Chloe turned to Jasmyn and Beatrice and motioned for them to smile. Their mouths curved up automatically, although they were still bug-eyed with fear.

"Remember, too, what being a cheerleader is all about," Coach Steele went on. "There is a poster in my office with the motto 'Competence, confidence, and community.' Competence means that you've worked hard to develop your skills. Confidence means that you believe in your-selves. And community means that you are here to sup-port our school, our fine athletes, and each other—and, of course, the many charities our organization helps out each year." She added, "Bottom line. Being a good cheerleader isn't just about physical ability. It's in here"—she pointed to her head—"and in here"—she pointed to her heart.

The gym broke out in wild applause. Coach Steele beamed. "Okay, it's time for me to get off the floor and for you to show us what you've got. Everyone please take a seat on the bleachers and wait for your number to be called. At this time, we're going to call numbers one through four to come out on the floor and do your cheers."

This is it, Chloe told herself.

❋

"Numbers five through eight, we'd like to see your dance now."

Chloe jogged off the floor along with numbers two through four: Leila Savett, Gemma Moore, and Phoebe Carter, respectively. The dance had gone well. She'd nailed the double pirouettes, and her relevés had been super-smooth. Now it was time to gear up for tumbling.

She passed Leila. "Good job," she said in a friendly voice.

Leila glanced away quickly and swiped her hand across her eyes. Her face was blotchy. Chloe realized that she was crying.

"What's wrong, Leila?" Chloe asked softly.

"As if you cared," Leila snapped.

"I *do* care. You can talk to me."

Leila crossed her arms over her chest. "I didn't sleep well last night because I was nervous about today," she confessed. "I'm tired and I'm not focused. I messed up my dance in a couple of spots. And for my cheer I actually did a *left* low half V first instead of a right. I am so stupid!" She started crying again.

"Aw." Chloe reached over and gave Leila a big hug. She hadn't seen Leila like this in a long, long time—not since she'd failed to advance to the Sunny Valley All-Stars elite team. And before that, it was when her pet hamster, Butterscotch, died. "Don't be so hard on yourself. We all mess up. Think positive! I saw your tumbling pass during clinics, and it was amazing! The judges are going to love it."

"Really?"

"Really."

Leila regarded Chloe suspiciously. "You're just saying this stuff. Deep down, you're probably glad I screwed up. It's less competition for you."

"*What?*"

Leila sniffed and turned to go.

"I know you didn't mean that. You're just upset," Chloe said as Leila started to walk away. "You're a great cheerleader, Leila. I hope you ace your tumbling and your stunt today. I know you will."

Leila hesitated, then kept walking. But Chloe could swear she heard her whisper: "Thanks, Chloe."

CHAPTER 20

"Number fifty, we'd like to see your running tumbling now."

Kate lined up against the wall and observed as one of the Varsity girls, Heather something, launched into a seamless round-off, back handspring, layout. She looked like a pro. Where had she learned to do that? There was no way Kate could come close to that kind of perfection.

The three judges bent over their notebooks and scribbled away. The one on the far left leaned across and whispered something to the others. No doubt they were giving Heather whatever-her-name-was a ton of points for that pass. She was probably already at the top of their Varsity list, and the tryouts weren't even over yet.

But Kate wasn't going for Varsity. She just wanted to make the JV squad again. *Stop psyching yourself out*, she told herself sternly.

"Number fifty-one, we'd like to see your running tumbling now."

Number fifty-one was Kalyn Min from the JV squad. Kate was next.

Kate's palms were sweaty, and her hands wouldn't stop shaking. She had to calm down in the next few seconds, or all would be lost.

She'd done really well so far in the tryouts. She'd aced the cheer and dance, and her toe touch, hurdler, Herkie, and pike had been nearly flawless, as had her back handspring.

But her running tumbling was worth up to ten points. And it was the element she felt the least sure of, despite hours of practice, not to mention the personal coaching session with Adam's sister Melissa.

As Kalyn threw her pass, Kate closed her eyes, massaged her temples, and rehearsed her own pass in her head.

She pictured herself running, then launching her round-off, and landing squarely on both feet with her hands by her ears.

She visualized swinging her arms down and up, pushing off her legs, and going into her back handspring.

Clean landing. Arms in front. Done!

"Number fifty-two, we'd like to see your running tumbling now."

Kate's eyes flew open. She felt dizzy and nauseated. Should she just bail before she made a complete fool of herself on the floor?

Someone touched her shoulder. She turned around; it was Chloe.

"You're okay," Chloe said with a firm nod. "You've got this!"

Kate nodded back. "Yes. I've got this."

Chloe patted her shoulder one last time and then gave her a gentle nudge.

Kate inhaled and exhaled quickly. Her heart raced like mad.

"I've got this," she repeated to herself. She stepped up to the edge of the floor.

She was aware of the judges watching her, their pens poised over their notebooks. Then she remembered what Coach Steele had told them earlier: *Have fun!*

Kate made herself smile. Not just smile, but *really* smile, as though she was goofing around in the backyard with Chloe, Emily, and Devin on a sunny afternoon.

She felt herself sprint across the floor, her feet sure and steady.

Round-off.

Back handspring.

Clean landing!

She stood up straight, being careful not to lock out her knees, and raised her arms in front of her. She was still smiling—this time, because she knew she'd nailed her pass. In fact, one of the judges actually smiled *back* at her before leaning over to whisper to the other two judges.

Yes!

Kate grinned from ear to ear as she jogged off the floor.

"Number fifty-three, we'd like to see your running tumbling now."

Chloe, Devin, and Emily were waiting for Kate by the bleachers. Chloe and Devin gave her high fives. Emily grabbed her in a fierce bear hug that practically knocked them both over.

Kate was delirious with relief.

Except…there was one more element to go. Their stunt.

❋

"Number one, we'd like to see your stunt now."

Chloe stepped forward along with Kate, Emily, and Devin.

"Please raise your hand if you're using this stunt for your tryout," one of the judges called.

All four girls raised their hands.

"Fine, thank you. Numbers one, five, twenty-two, and fifty-two, please proceed with your stunt."

Kate and her friends got into their positions for the ground-up liberty. Devin placed her right hand on Emily's right ankle and her left hand under Emily's seat. Chloe held Emily's right foot while Kate assisted with that grip and also supported her wrist.

"One, two, down, up!" All four girls dipped slightly on the word *down*, and on the word *up*, Emily shot up to a lib position, her arms in a V.

The other three extended through and fixed their gazes up at Emily.

A few seconds later, they dismounted neatly and smiled at the audience. Several people cheered and clapped.

"Omigosh, we did it!" Emily whispered as they trotted off the floor.

"I think that was worth a perfect score, don't you?" Chloe said excitedly.

They sat down on the bleachers and toweled off their faces. Kate couldn't believe she was done. *Done!* All four of them were, in fact.

Jasmyn and Beatrice performed their extension prep stunt a few minutes later, along with two classmates from their middle school. Kate squeezed Chloe's hand as they all watched with bated breath. Chloe's eyes were glued to her girls, who were both bases, as they squatted down along with the back spot to raise their top girl in the air.

One . . . two . . .

The top went up and then extended neatly as Jasmyn, Beatrice, and their back spot supported her.

Chloe punched her fist in the air. "*Yes!* They did it!"

"Is it just me, or does anyone else think Chloe is going to be a cheerleading coach someday?" Emily joked.

Devin and Kate both raised their hands. All four girls burst into laughter.

Kate reached for her water bottle and took a thirsty sip as they continued watching the other stunt groups. Now, it was just a matter of waiting for everyone to finish.

Then waiting for the judges to add up their scores.

Then waiting for Coach Steele to make her final decisions about who would make JV and who would make Varsity.

How would it all turn out? Would Kate be on the JV squad again? Would Chloe and Emily rise to Varsity?

And what about Devin? With the Logans' offer before her, would she even *be* a cheerleader next year?

CHAPTER 21

"Thank you all for coming out!" Coach Steele said loudly as everyone put on their warm-up jackets and prepared to leave. "Tryouts went great today. We'll be posting the results on the outside of the gym doors in a couple of hours, so please come back then."

She added: "A final word. I wish we could take everyone who tried out. As it is, we can't even choose the top forty or so candidates. You might be better skill-wise or experience-wise than someone else, but we have to think of the whole. We can't form squads out of just tops or just bases or just back spots. We have to go with the best combination of the three. Our job is to create teams, not collections of talented individuals."

Devin leaned over to ask Chloe a question about the posting of the results when she felt her phone vibrating in her jacket pocket. She glanced at the clock behind the backboard. It was ten minutes to six. She'd promised her answer to the Logans no later than six PM so they could submit a final list of competitors to the Southern California Superstars Gymnastics Tournament.

"Next Monday, there will be a mandatory meeting for the new JV and Varsity squads at seven PM," Coach Steele went on. "We'll discuss practice schedules, summer camp, our rules and regs, and other important details. Your parents are welcome to join us. In fact, we would *like* for them to be here, if possible, so they can sign forms and so forth. But now…go home, have some dinner, and we'll see you back around eight!"

Devin and her friends grabbed their duffel bags and shuffled through the double doors together. Devin's phone vibrated again. She slipped her hand into her jacket pocket and palmed it distractedly.

"How do you all think you did?" Emily asked the others.

"I'm not sure. I *felt* good. But like Coach Steele said, she can't pick the best individual cheerleaders. It's like she has to put together the pieces of a really complicated puzzle," Chloe replied.

"*Two* puzzles," Kate pointed out.

"Yes. Two puzzles. The JV puzzle and the Varsity puzzle. Devin, how do you think you did?" Chloe asked.

Devin was silent.

"Hey! Earth to Devin!" Emily elbowed her gently.

"What?" Devin perked up. "Yeah. I was just thinking. The Logans have left me, like, three messages. I told them I'd let them know my answer by six. It's almost six now."

"How can you give them your answer? You won't even know the results for two more hours," Emily reminded her.

Devin nodded. "Yeah, I know."

"Well? What's your decision?" Chloe demanded.

"Guys! Maybe Devin hasn't decided yet. We should give her some space," Kate piped up.

"Actually, I *have* decided," Devin announced.

She stopped abruptly in the middle of the hallway. The flow of foot traffic swarmed around her and her friends. "Good job today!" Jenn Hoffheimer called out as she and a bunch of other JV cheerleaders exited to the parking lot, smiling and waving.

Devin waved back, feeling three pairs of eyes boring into her.

"So what's your decision?" Chloe repeated.

"Okay, here goes. I love cheerleading—" Devin began.

"Oh. My. *Gawd.* That means she's leaving us!" Emily practically yelled.

Devin held up her hand. "Let me finish. I love cheerleading. I didn't really realize it until this week, when we went through the clinics and tryouts. *Especially* when the four of us nailed that ground-up liberty! And even though I'm seriously tempted by the Logans' offer, I'm not ready to give up being a cheerleader just yet. I want to stay with it for at least one more year and see where it takes me. So I'm going to call the Logans and tell them no. After all, I can always rethink my decision next spring."

"*Yay!*" Chloe, Emily, and Kate began jumping up and down.

Emily stopped and grabbed Devin's arm. "Wait! So you're going to call them now, before you find out if you made the cut or not?"

"I promised them an answer, so, yeah," Devin replied. "If I don't make the squad...well, I can always do something else my sophomore year. Maybe I'll join Mateo's scuba diving club," she joked.

"This is so awesome! *Beyond* awesome! Pizzas are on me tonight!" Emily announced. "Actually, they're on my parents. My dad just texted and said we could all come over and have dinner at my house. Then he and my mom will drive us back here for the results."

"Pizza! *Yes!*" Devin couldn't imagine anything she wanted more right now. After a long, hard day of classes, tryouts, and making epic decisions about her future, she couldn't think of a better way to chill than having some pepperoni slices with her three best friends.

She smiled to herself. *Her three best friends.* She'd never thought of Chloe, Emily, and Kate that way before. And of course, there was Mateo, too.

After nine months in Sunny Valley, she was finally letting people into her life.

She really *was* growing up.

❋

After dinner, Mr. and Mrs. Arellano drove Emily, Devin, Chloe, and Kate back to Northside. Devin's mom was already there, along with Mr. and Mrs. Davis and Mr. MacDonald. Jasmyn and Beatrice were there with their parents as well. So were Kate's boyfriend, Adam, and their friend Willow.

The hallway outside the gym was jam-packed. Most of the students who'd tried out had brought their friends and families with them, too. Everyone had their phones and cameras out, ready to capture the big moment.

Devin glanced quickly at the gym doors. The list wasn't up yet.

"Coach Steele said eight, right? It's eight now," Devin said impatiently.

"I...can't...stand...the...suspense," Emily moaned.

Adam and Willow came up to Kate. "Are you okay?" Adam asked Kate as he slipped his arm around her shoulder.

"I'm nervous," Kate admitted.

"You probably rocked your stupid audition, and you're just being modest," Willow said with an eye-roll.

"*Tryout*," Kate corrected her.

The gym doors opened suddenly and Coach Steele emerged. She looked exhausted, but her eyes were as alert as always.

Coach Steele held up two pieces of paper and taped one on each door. "The list on the left is our new JV squad. The list on the right is Varsity. There are no names, just numbers. Twenty-two per squad, including two alternates. Good luck, everybody—and thank you again for all your hard work!" With that, she disappeared back into the gym.

Everyone began moving toward the doors at once. Leila was at the front of the mob. "I MADE JV!" she screamed after a moment. Mr. and Mrs. Savett raised their cameras high and clicked away.

More students took a look at the lists. Some pumped their fists in the air or hugged their friends and family. Others burst into tears or walked away with their heads hung low.

"I don't want to see," Kate whispered to her friends.

"I don't, either," Chloe replied. "Let's just go back to Emily's and have some more pizza."

"Chlo! We have to make a pact right here, right now. If one of us makes Varsity and the other one doesn't, we'll still be BFFs," Emily said.

"Pinkie swear!" Chloe promised, holding up her hand.

"Pinkie swear," Emily agreed. The two of them hooked their little fingers solemnly.

The four girls eventually got to the front of the line. "I know! Let's all close our eyes, and we'll look at the lists on the count of three," Emily suggested.

Kate nodded. "Good idea!"

Devin closed her eyes. She heard Chloe count: "One, two, three!"

They opened their eyes at once. Devin stared at the lists, her heart pounding in her chest.

There she was. Number twenty-two.

She had made the JV squad.

"*Yes!*" she cried out.

"Congratulations, sweetie," her mother said, holding up her phone to take a picture.

"Number one! I made JV!" Chloe said excitedly.

"Omigosh, me too!" Kate exclaimed.

"Wow. Me too. Number five," Emily said. She sounded a little disappointed.

"We're proud of you, *mija*," Mrs. Arellano said, wrapping her arms around Emily and planting a kiss on her cheek. "You worked hard. You should feel very good about that."

"*Oh...my...gosh!*"

Jasmyn and Beatrice were standing just behind Devin and the others. Jasmyn began crying. Beatrice did, too.

Devin glanced again at the lists. Had they not made the cut?

"Seventeen and twenty-one! You guys, you *made* it!

We're gonna be squad mates!" Chloe yelled. "Congratulations!" She began crying, too.

Jasmyn and Beatrice threw themselves at Chloe and sobbed into her shoulders, overwhelmed with happy tears. Devin got misty-eyed just watching them.

Her phone buzzed. Was it the Logans again? She'd called them earlier and informed them of her decision. She'd also thanked them for their incredible generosity and kindness. They'd been very gracious about her decision and wished her luck with cheerleading. What could they want now?

But it wasn't the Logans. It was Mateo.

"Hello?" Devin said, pressing her phone to her ear.

"Hey, it's me! I'm sorry I couldn't get over there. My mom had to stay late at work, so I'm stuck at home with the Samster. What's going on?" he asked eagerly.

"I made JV!" Devin told him.

"Wow, congratulations! That's amazing. Is that what you wanted?"

"Yes. It's *exactly* what I wanted," Devin said, meaning it.

"Awesome. Congratulations again. We can celebrate at the Lobster Claw. And the spring dance. That is, if you'll go to the spring dance with me?"

"Of course!" Devin said happily.

Could this day get any better?

CHAPTER 22

For once, Emily actually *missed* Nadine.

It was Saturday afternoon, and she and Zoe were working at Rockabella without their boss. Nadine had slipped out for a couple of hours to visit the studio of a local designer whose clothes she was thinking of carrying at the store. Emily was not enjoying being alone with Zoe, who seemed to want to rub her face in the fact that she hadn't made Varsity. When-slash-why-slash-how did Emily ever think that Zoe was a nice person?

"So!" Zoe smiled smugly as she stood at the counter, stringing silver-and-rhinestone earrings on a jewelry tree.

"If you'd listened to me, you'd be a Varsity hotshot instead of a lowly JV. I was even going to teach you the tryout cheer and dance *before* clinics, so that you'd have a head start."

"You know what, Zoe? I'm really happy with how things turned out, and I'm proud to be on the JV squad again," Emily replied as she hung up a new shipment of skirts. She tried to keep her voice calm and even so she wouldn't reveal how much Zoe had hurt and disappointed her over the past few weeks. "Besides, it was almost impossible to make Varsity for next year. None of the current Varsity girls got cut. There were only two possible spots, and two really talented sophomores from JV got them."

She didn't add that Coach Steele hadn't made Varsity, either. That job had been given to Mr. Piretti—now *Coach* Piretti.

Zoe had mentioned once that Coach Piretti and Principal Cilento were good friends. Emily couldn't help thinking that maybe Principal Cilento had used his influence to ensure that his good friend was hired for the Varsity position.

The front door opened. Braden walked in.

"Omigosh, hi!" Emily said, waving. She hadn't seen him since before tryouts.

"Emily! Hey!" He smiled and waved back. Today, he wore a cream polo shirt, board shorts, and flip-flops. Could he be cuter?

"Braden!" Zoe rushed up to Braden and threw her arms around his neck. "It's been ages! How are you?" she gushed.

Emily blanched. What was Zoe doing, flinging herself at Braden like that? Did they have a history together?

Braden pulled Zoe's hands from his neck and stepped back with a confused expression. "Hey, Zoe. Nice to see you, too. Is my mom around?"

"Actually, she's—" Emily began.

"She stepped out, but she'll be back," Zoe cut in. "Is there something I can help you with? You look like you could use a pick-me-up. Do you want to go down the street and grab a cappuccino?" she added, flipping her long platinum hair over her shoulders.

"That's sweet, but no, thanks. Hey, Emily, do you have a minute?" Braden asked.

Emily could barely suppress a smile of triumph. *Take that, Zoe!* "Sure!"

Zoe glared at Emily. "Actually, you can't. Take a minute, that is. There's a huge pile of dresses to steam. Nadine wanted them all done by the time she gets back."

"I did them already," Emily announced. "So, what did you want to talk to me about, Braden?"

Zoe scowled and disappeared into the back room.

Braden turned to Emily. "I haven't seen you in a while. How's it going?"

"Good! I made the JV squad again for next year!"

"Well done!"

"Thanks. Did you hear back from your colleges?"

"Yes! Good news on that front. I got into USC! I was wait-listed at first, but just yesterday I found out that I'm off the wait list."

"Wow, congratulations!" Emily told him. She reminded herself to add USC to the list of her prospective colleges when she was a junior.

"Thanks. Oh, and by the way . . . didn't you tell me that you're on some committee at your school for a dance?"

"Yup. The spring dance."

"What day is that, anyway?"

Emily stared at him. Where was this line of questioning going?

"Um . . . Saturday, May third. Seven o'clock. You—I mean, *people*—from other schools are totally welcome to come! People including you, that is," she rambled on awkwardly.

"Great! I might bring some friends and stop by. Can you give me your number in case I need to text you? To ask you for more information?"

"Sure!"

As Emily typed her number into Braden's phone, she thought that she might have a reason to wear that teal dress to the dance, after all.

❋

Later that night, Emily and Chloe had a sleepover at the Arellanos' house—just the two of them.

Dressed in their PJs, they sat on the living room floor surfing channels and eating big bowls of Mocha Fudge Madness ice cream. Emily had gone kind of crazy with the whipped cream and sprinkles, but it was okay. It was Saturday night, and tryouts were finally behind them. They could relax a little.

"Why would anyone watch a movie about sharks attacking a ski resort?" Chloe mused, pointing the remote at the TV.

"Seriously? That's *Snow Shark*, one of my favorite movies of all time. You've got to watch it, especially the part where there's a blizzard and sharks fall from the sky and eat the unsuspecting skiers!"

"*Eww.* That makes me *really* not want to finish this ice cream."

Emily laughed. "Sorry!"

Chloe laughed, too. "It's okay. Soooo...where's Chris tonight?"

"Your BF? He's out with his friend Quinn again. By the way, Quinn *did* dump her BF, Fernando. So it doesn't look good for the two of you—you and Chris, I mean," Emily clarified.

"Stop that! He is *not* my BF. He's a senior. Plus, he's your brother, which means that he's kind of like *my* brother," Chloe pointed out.

"Yes to that last part. As for him being a senior...well, I kind of like a senior, too," Emily confessed.

"What?" Chloe sat up and hit the Mute button. "Spill!"

"His name's Braden. He's Nadine's son. And, unfortunately, he goes to Breckenridge. But not for long!" Emily added hastily. "He just got into USC for this fall."

"That's cool! What's he like?"

Emily described him to Chloe. "It's probably not going anywhere, but it's still fun to flirt," she finished. "Somehow, now that we're practically sophomores, it feels okay to notice older boys. Do you know what I mean?"

Chloe grinned. "I know *exactly* what you mean."

They stared in silence at the muted TV screen as fake snow mingled with equally fake sharks showered down upon a mountain chalet. After a moment, Emily turned to Chloe. "I know what would go really well with this movie. Two words. 'Mani-pedis!'"

"Yes!"

"Or is 'mani-pedi' one word?"

"I have no idea. Let's grab the supplies and debate the grammar later."

"Okay." Emily paused. "Hey, Chloe?"

"Hmm?"

"Are you okay about not making Varsity?"

Chloe held up her hand and studied her fingernails. "Yes," she said finally. "I'm totally okay about not making Varsity. Because now I get to be on the squad with you and

Devin and Kate for another year. And we've got some awesome new teammates, too, like Jasmyn and Beatrice."

Emily nodded. "That's exactly how I feel."

Chloe glanced up and smiled at Emily. Emily smiled back.

"Mani-pedi supplies," Chloe reminded Emily.

"Right away!"

Emily jumped to her feet and headed upstairs, humming and bopping her head.

Things were finally back to normal.

Actually, they were way *better* than normal.

CHAPTER 23

On the night of the spring dance, Chloe stood in the open doorway of the gym and marveled at the amazing transformation. Glittering green and yellow streamers hung from the rafters. White crepe paper and mason jars full of tulips covered the tables. A disco ball shimmered from above and cast glittery diamond light across the wooden floor, which was packed wall-to-wall with people dancing.

And best of all, the Cupcake Zombies were rocking the stage with a song called "My Undead Romance." Chloe and Emily had picked *the* perfect band for the occasion.

Chloe gazed out at the sea of dancers. Kate was with

Adam. The two of them looked incredibly happy together. Devin was with Mateo; they looked pretty cozy, too.

Chloe also spotted most of the girls from the JV squad, including Leila, who was dancing with a basketball player named Jamal. She didn't see Chris Arellano, though, or Chris's friend Quinn.

Oh, well.

"Chlo!"

Chloe turned. Emily was hurrying in her direction. She wore a pretty teal dress and matching heels that made her wobble slightly, especially since she was practically speed walking. As she approached, she took pictures of the dancers with her shiny new phone, which she'd bought with the money she'd made at Rockabella. Her boss, Nadine, had apparently given her extra hours, on Sundays, which had helped Emily replace Chad more quickly than she had expected.

"Hey, Em. What's up? When did you become the event photographer?" Chloe asked.

"Chloe, we have a problem! We may be running out of punch! There's, like, way more people than we expected. Everyone seems to have shown up at the last minute. I think Gena Showalter could have done a better job with the advance ticket sales, don't you?" Emily sniped.

"Why do you care whether there's enough punch? You weren't on the punch subcommittee or whatever," Chloe pointed out.

"I know! But I'm used to being in charge, to organizing it all. The one time I cut back, everything goes wrong!"

"Like what?"

"Like—uh—there might not be enough punch. And the tablecloths should have been yellow, not white."

Chloe put her hands on Emily's shoulders. "You know what? There'll be plenty of punch. And the tablecloths look fine. Besides, you *did* your job already. You and I picked an awesome band. Subcommittee of two, remember? So now it's time for us to chill and enjoy the dance."

"Yeah, but how?"

"Excuse me. Emily?"

A cute guy walked up to them. Chloe gaped at him. *Cute* wasn't quite the right word. More like *hot. Insanely hot.*

"Braden! You showed up!" Emily exclaimed.

Braden grinned. "I did. I brought some of my friends, too. I'd introduce you, but they're already out on the dance floor. Hey, do you want to dance? Or are you busy with your committee stuff? Love your dress, by the way."

Emily batted her eyelashes at him. "Thanks! And no, I am *so* not busy! In fact, I was just saying to my friend Chloe here, I have absolutely nothing to do!"

"Great. Hey, Chloe, I'm Braden. It's nice to meet you. Do you mind if I borrow Emily for a minute?"

"Not at all," Chloe trilled. "You two have fun!"

Chloe watched as Braden led Emily onto the dance floor. Emily turned briefly, pointed to Braden, and mouthed the words *What do you think?*

Chloe fanned her face and pretended to faint. Emily laughed.

Just then, someone tapped Chloe on the shoulder.

Chloe glanced up. It was Chris, looking impossibly handsome in a black polo and dark jeans.

Her breath caught in her throat.

But it's just Chris, she reminded herself. *Emily's big brother!*

"Oh! Hey! You just missed Emily!" she sputtered.

"Yeah. I texted to see if she needed me to give her a ride later. She didn't answer. I think she's still getting used to her new phone."

"You want me to give her the message? I think she's, uh, busy."

"Sure. Thanks." Chris glanced at the stage. "You having fun?"

"Yes! I love this band, don't you?"

"They're awesome. Eddie's friends with Nikita. She's the drummer. Hey, do you want to dance?"

Chloe blinked. Her heart thumped in her chest. Had Chris Arellano just asked her to dance?

"Come on!" Chris grabbed her hand and pulled her

from her spot. "I love this song. 'The Infinite Adventure'—do you know it?"

And then, just like that, Chloe was swaying on the dance floor with the most popular senior boy at Northside High. The boy who used to tease her and Emily when they were little. Who used to hide their poms all over the house.

Chloe knew they would probably never be more than friends. Still, just for tonight, she was having the time of her life.

❋

The following afternoon, Chloe, Emily, Devin, and Kate lay on the warm sand at La Paz Beach and stared up at the bright blue sky. Kate's parents were nearby, splashing in the water with her little siblings, Garrett, Jack, and Sasha.

Kate sat up and unzipped her family's massive cooler, which contained their lunch, snacks, and beverages. She pulled out four bottles of water, kept one for herself, and passed the rest around to her friends.

As she sipped her water, she thought about the poem Willow had written for her last month. It had actually come true. Kate used to have a hard time believing she was a good cheerleader. She'd even been afraid she wouldn't survive tryouts.

But she'd not only survived. She'd outdone herself and changed the course of her fate.

And now, she was excited about the future, especially her future with Adam. With her friends. With cheerleading.

"This…is…perfection," Emily declared as a wave rolled in and tickled their toes. "We should do this, like, all the time."

"Yeah. If only we didn't have class," Chloe said, slipping on her shades.

"Or homework," Kate added.

"Or practice," Devin piped up. "Actually, no. I'd love it if my schedule consisted of nothing but cheerleading and the beach!"

"I thought you hated the beach," Kate said as she reached for the sunscreen.

"No, I just hate going in the water. Although I'm kinda getting used to it. Mateo's been a good influence. He always says that the only way to overcome your fears is by doing the things you're afraid of."

"You know what, guys? Two words. *Summer vacation,*" Emily said. "That's exactly what we'll have this summer. Cheerleading and the beach."

"Devin, wait till you come to cheer camp with us. It's the best!" Chloe gushed.

"You guys went together last summer, right?" Devin asked.

Chloe grinned. "Right. And it was a blast. Although I have a funny feeling this year's gonna be even better."

"To summer!" Kate said, raising her bottle of water in the air.

Chloe, Emily, and Devin raised their bottles, too. "To summer!" they toasted.